selective

memory

The Depth of Emotion Series, Book Two

D.D. LORENZO

selective memory
Book Two in the Depth of Emotion series

Copyright © 2014, 2017 by D.D. Lorenzo
Cover design by Regina Wamba, Mae I Design
Editing by Connie Miconi, Lucky 13
Formatting and Interior Design by JT Formatting

Library of Congress Cataloging-in-Publication Data

Lorenzo, D.D.
Selective Memory (Depth of Emotion series) – 2nd edition
ISBN-13: 978-0-9912359-1-9

For Mike.

Always.

*T*hank you for allowing me into your world. I would like to have you be a part of mine. At the end of this book you will find a note from me to you, as well as an easy way that we can keep in touch.

Happy reading!

Marisol *Prologue*

*T*he building was perfect; after all, anything less wouldn't do. A view of the sea because he liked it; seclusion, because it was critical for her plan to succeed. It wasn't a sizeable house, but it was adequate for her needs. He would believe that she had kept his likes in mind. It was all about illusion, as most things were.

Her heels clicked on the polished hardwood as she ascended the stairs like a queen. All that she wanted would play out within these walls; no detail had been overlooked. The plan was in motion, but as in all things, time ruled success.

And success she would have.

Chapter 1

DECLAN

I relished the burn at the back of my throat. It had become an almost nightly ritual, albeit a bit masochistic. After filling the day with business, my schedule now allowed me time to think. This part of the day was the beginning of my struggle—that beautiful time when the sun slowly sinks over the bay. A window of minutes and hours when color would filter back into my black and white life.

I despised it.

Everything in The Studio spoke of Aria's influence. Her presence called out to me from the layout of the rooms, to the selection of the furniture. I tilted the full bottle of Jameson to my glass of flashbacks, more than generous with my portion. The whiskey was both a blessing and a curse, much like I had allowed every other aspect of my life to become. Its potion helped me to dull the pain in my body, but exacerbated the gaping hole in my heart. I missed her.

It had taken months of grueling therapy to function at anything near normal capacity; and still, I struggled with my gait. I no longer saw myself as I once did. The days of being a male supermodel were gone; who would want a disfigured man representing their company? The public was fickle. The industry wanted and expected perfection—something I no longer was by anyone's standards.

I placed the tumbler to my lips, closed my eyes, and swallowed.

It was an attempt to both anesthetize myself and shut out the world. Unfortunately, each day the routine rendered the same painful result—images of Aria flooded me. Scenes of loving her seared my mind and I leaned into the burn. As the whiskey dulled my effort to resist, I allowed myself to be swept away into the dreams. The ebony waves in her dark curls caught the moonlight as her hair cascaded down her back. The bend of her throat toyed with me and ignited my desire as I remembered how her back arched against me. I could almost feel her body fall into mine. I took a deep breath, my chest expanding as the memories hit me full force. I could almost smell the intoxicating fragrance she wore. I leaned back in my chair as I imagined feeling her curves against me. A simultaneous mixture of torture and bliss, I didn't have to take responsibility for thinking of her while permitting the drink its effects. I lost myself in her during this torturous part of the day. The solitude that I was afforded once business wound down and no one dared enter my office let me fall helplessly into the effects of the whiskey and an abyss of memories with my beautiful girl. How did I let things get so far out of control?

Aria had offered unconditional support and unwavering love. I convinced myself that by pushing her away, both physically and emotionally, I was doing her a favor. She deserved better than what I had become because I would never be the same person. The doctors warned me that I could have physical issues in the future. My body had been no match for the vehicle that hit me. All I could think at the time was that I couldn't subject her to a future filled with uncertainty. She had already been through enough. Loving a man who was always in physical pain was no way for a beautiful woman to live, especially Aria. She deserved better. I was the one who had decided that she would be better off without me.

The plan started to form the moment I woke from surgery. Without fail, Aria was with me every day. She never wanted to leave me, even when visiting hours were over. I had mixed emotions about her being there. The selfish part of me wanted Aria around because she was hopeful. Then an image from the accident would appear to distort my thoughts. I would turn into a bastard and angrily lash out at her, blaming her because I remembered that she had run away from me when she promised not to. I couldn't help the feelings of resentment that came from deep inside once they made their way to the surface. I became bitter and hateful. She would extend kindness and I would respond by barking some antagonistic retort. My cyclonic moods and the tears that followed created a never-ending circle of pain, so I made a decision—I would drive her away. It didn't take too long to destroy a love that was already fractured. One day, after a visit in which she completely broke down, she didn't come to see me anymore. My brother told me that Aria had a breakdown. She took the blame for the accident upon herself. I knew then that I'd done my part to convince her that she was the guilty party. I listened as Carter lashed out at me, calling me a "self-centered bastard" and a "righteous son-of-a-bitch." I was rabid in my verbal assault and said that Aria was better off without me. Carter also told me that if I weren't his brother, he would have left me to fend for myself. I deserved every accusation, but I had accomplished my goal. I drove her away.

Since then, I hadn't let my guard down. I lived in a constant state of preparation, bracing myself for another wave to hit. The emotions were overwhelming. Loneliness and desperation were a black hole that threatened to suck me in, even on my best days. Since my faith wouldn't permit me to kill myself, I did the next best thing—I committed emotional suicide. No longer would I allow myself to feel—functioning would have to suffice. I wouldn't allow anyone to get close to me ever again. I followed the doctor's advice, doing whatever was necessary for the hopes of keeping my body marketable, if that was even possible. Relationships would be solely for gain. There would be no more indulging in thoughts of love. I wouldn't allow it. One woman had held my heart. I had no desire to compare what I had with her to anything I might have again. Aria was the only woman to have held that portion of me, and that space was now locked away.

As I threw back the remaining contents of my glass, I knew that this, too, would have to stop. Eventually, I would need to give up the daily moments when reminders of my life with Aria sliced through my determination due to the effects of the alcohol. I would miss it. It was the only sliver of pleasure in an otherwise void day. The colors of the sunset, combined with the whiskey, brought warmth to my cold spirit. However, to survive without her, it was imperative to annihilate the connection to my emotions. That time would come soon enough; but for today, I could blame my weaknesses on the whiskey.

Aria

Chapter

2

old, crisp air filled my lungs. It was the invigorating type of air that burned your nose as you breathed it in, yet made you feel alive. Walking on the beach had become a blessing and a curse. It used to be the activity that gave me peace, but now it also held painful memories. Yoga had replaced my simple walks as it currently provided more of the calm feelings, while running helped me to conquer the monsters that entered my thoughts unbidden. I would never again want to escape them, for I had spent enough time fleeing from subconscious ghosts. Over the past few months, I had discovered how strong a woman I could be. Monsters and ghosts were the least of my problems.

I had retreated too much over the past year or so. I had fled from the overwhelming enormity of death into the arms of my beloved ocean. It called to me, its waves giving me unexplained peace. It was the one constant in my life. As unpredictable as my recent life events had been, the sea could always be trusted to be there, waiting for me. Its energy was the source from which I drew my strength. I felt so small and insignificant when I stood before the expanse of its blue beauty. The sand embraced me the moment it felt my weight. Gritty beige granules caressed me when I placed my foot on its welcome mat. I knew I belonged here. I couldn't escape the hold that the sea had on me; not ever, and not because of him.

I was going for a run earlier than normal this morning because thoughts of him had kept me awake. Sometimes they were pleasant memories and other times cruel nightmares. I had learned to give in to them when they came; and because I had done so, they tortured me less and less. Declan would always be a part of me; I had come to accept this and even to embrace it. If I were truthful, I would admit to letting myself drift toward thoughts of him purposefully at times.

As he was recovering from his accident, I tortured myself unmercifully, blaming myself for his injury. I wasn't alone—he blamed me as well. Months went by, and try as hard as I might, I was unsuccessful at lifting Declan up, mentally or physically. As I watched him drown in misery, I became helpless. I was so in love with him that I clung tightly and I let him drag me down with him. Sinking lower and lower, we succumbed so far into the depths of his despair that I was no longer recognizable. I lost myself. I would only breathe when he chose to inhale and his depression finally suffocated me. My spirit died under the weight of his monotonous pessimism. I fought to make him better, but it only proved to make me worse. As much as it broke my heart, after an afternoon of his constant berating and belittling of us both, I removed myself from his life.

One of our physicians, Doctor Dulaney, was in the hallway when I left Declan's room that horrible afternoon. She could see that I was upset, was losing weight, and wasn't recovering well. When the doctor invited me to sit for a few minutes, she coaxed me into revealing the source of the problem. Through tears, I confessed that I wanted to help him, but didn't know how. Doctor Dulaney, with the most sincere expression on her face, told me that I needed to allow Declan to work through this alone.

She gave me the name of a doctor that she believed could help me through the trauma of witnessing Declan's accident. At the time, I didn't think anyone could help, but once I met with Doctor Sumner, my opinion changed.

Over the next few months, Doctor Sumner helped me to see that

Declan's accident was just that—an accident. I wasn't to blame. I was in love and had reacted with a natural instinct when I saw the man I loved with another woman. "Fight or flight," Doctor Sumner had said. Anxiety and adrenaline were what had caused me to run. Intellectually, I knew that there was an explanation for why Marisol was with Declan, but we had just argued the day before about her. The doctor assured me that I was normal, but the situation was not. Once I overcame that hurdle, I stopped beating myself up and began to recover. The physical exertion of running helped the emotional healing and yoga helped me to center my thoughts.

I felt stronger in mind and body. One thing was certain— Marisol would NEVER take me down again. I would see her in hell first! Declan was another matter entirely. As far as he was concerned, we were over; but I still had much to say. I hadn't yet decided how it would happen. One day. We had to recover individually.

As I stood in the sunlight, I could feel the healing taking place. Just as the cold cleansed my lungs, it washed my mind clean of unhealthy thoughts. I was once again running my business and doing very well. Work kept me busy. The baby boomers all wanted to retire to the beach, so I was rehabbing quite a few homes. I loved my little house. While it didn't sit right on the beach like Declan's, it was close enough that I could run on the boardwalk every day. I loved the quaint shops and restaurants. All of my friends lived between here and where I used to live with Declan. We could get together within an hour's drive. I felt well enough to get together with the girls twice for lunch and shopping. The first time, we met at Dos Locos and everyone except for Aimee seemed to be walking on eggshells, afraid to talk to me about Declan. He was the "elephant in the room."

"So how are you feeling, sweetie?" Aimee's was the first voice that greeted me.

"I'm good; really good." I could tell that they were taking a mental inventory.

Katherine placed her handbag on the table and then gave me a warm smile.

"You look buff. Like you've been working out."

"Yep. Taking charge of my health."

"How's your appetite? Have you been sleeping?" Aimee waved over the waiter as she waited for me to answer the rapid-fire questions. I took a deep breath, my eyes wide because I hadn't expected the interrogation.

"I'm just fine." A smirk filled my lips.*" I smirked. "I do feel like I need a drink now."*

"Oh, honey." Aimee was instantly repentant. *"I didn't mean it like that. It's just that everyone worries about you."*

Paige immediately came to my defense. *"I think she looks damn good."*

"I think you look good too, Aria," Katherine chimed in. *"I wish I could have done more to help."*

I reached over to pat her hand. *"It's okay. Sometimes, you have to go through stuff on your own, you know?"* I shrugged. *"There just isn't any way around it, girls. The tough stuff is what makes you grow. Besides, you really wouldn't have wanted to see me. I looked kind of rough there for a while."*

"No rougher than lover boy looks," Aimee mumbled under her breath, causing Paige and Katherine to throw her deadly glares. She shrugged her shoulders, giving all of us a defensive look. *"What? You both know it's true."* Aimee shrugged and gave all of us a defensive look. *"Don't you think it's better that she knows on the chance that she sees him?"*

I hadn't expected Declan and me to be the topic of conversation, but I also wanted to diffuse an uncomfortable, escalating atmosphere. *"Okay, stop. All of you."* I put both palms up. *"I know how Declan is, and he isn't my concern anymore. Let's move on."* The action silenced all three of them. If they were waiting for more of an explanation, I wasn't offering any. After an uncomfortable, pregnant pause, I continued. *"I say martinis are in order; wouldn't you agree? A little liquid diffusing of the tension—on me."* I ordered a *round of drinks and still no one was talking. "I'm not made of glass, you know." Again, no one spoke. "Oh, c'mon. I went through a tough time and had a breakdown. I'm over it. You all need to just let it go."*

Our server brought the drinks and they continued to be hesitant. It was making me uncomfortable. I treasured these women. They were each part of my recovery. They had called, stopped by, walked with me, brought meals, watched movies, made me laugh, and even handed me Kleenex. I took a sip of my drink and decided that I would break the ice. "Okay, I'll go first. The breakdown was long overdue. To hear my doctor explain it, two very emotional events, within a very short period, were too much for me. The death of my father and feeling responsible for Declan's accident were two massive traumas. I bottled everything up. According to Doctor Sumner, my day of reckoning was the day I broke down on the beach."

Aimee, usually the most outspoken, but also the most tenderhearted, was the first to speak. "Do you miss him?"

"Aimee!" Without missing a beat, Paige's and Katherine's objection came out in unison. I put my hand up. I didn't need protection.

"Yes," I answered. I took another sip. The chocolate added some sweetness to my bitter admission.

"We won't talk about him for the rest of lunch," Paige said. "There are other topics of discussion."

"You're sweet. There are other things that we could talk about, but this is the one that we'll keep dancing around. I'm stronger than you think I am. And I'm getting stronger every day." I looked down into my drink as I sipped again. I licked my lips and chuckled. "I might need another one of these to get through this, but as long as one of you is driving me home, fire away."

On that day, the conversation had been painful, but necessary. As I took the first steps in my run, I realized how lucky I am. I have the sun on my face and the wind in my hair—and Declan out of my life.

Chapter 3

DECLAN

eclan...

Aria whispered in my ear, her beautiful face a mist of memory in my semi-conscious state. Then the terror in her eyes became unmistakable. I wanted to reach out to her, but my arms weren't long enough, my feet not swift enough, and my mind not clear enough. An impotent helplessness overcame me as I slept. I wanted to protect her; but in truth, she was my strength. Frustration had me bound. The space and time between us were a hindrance to Aria's safety. The parameters of delusion dictated my movements and I opened my mouth to speak. Only one word came out and its sound was in slow motion. The effort to call her was impossible because of some incredible, forceful energy. It nearly slew me as I stared at her. Terror ripped from my throat as air abandoned my lungs.

AAAA...RRRIII...AAAAAA!!!

Paralyzed at the sight of her standing on the street, I telepathically willed her actions. In what seemed an eternity, my eyes shifted downward. The slight motion of her steps, one delicate foot after the other, liquidated and floated in my delusion. Her legs transformed before my eyes back to a solid form as she placed her feet onto the curb and out of harm's way. The recurring nightmare, a constant source of agony, continued until I was content with the sight of her away from the street. Momentarily, I felt peace. I drifted in relief and contentment, sailing away. Then, for a fraction of an instant, the tension eased and my lungs filled with air. I knew all would be well.

GO!

With the word, the effects of the impact registered excruciating pain in my lower back and the torturous feeling made me rise in my bed. Hot, searing coals split my skin and filled the middle of my spine. Molten and jagged, they liquidated and flowed throughout my spinal cord and downward into my sacrum. The agony plugged the voids and spaces where a whole and healthy limb once resided. The misery claimed me over and over, as the nightmare victimized me once again.

My eyes flew open. Anguished, my breath came in short, desperate gasps. I gripped at the bed sheet for something—anything—to hold. I didn't want to acknowledge that I wanted and needed Aria beside me on nights like these. As the mirage faded and reality settled in, my eyes focused on the ceiling. Slowly and purposefully, I breathed, reminding myself that I only needed to follow the instructions Aria had given me so many times in the hospital.

"Just three deep breaths, baby. Three. Deep. Breaths."

If I concentrated, I could almost hear her sweet, lyrical voice, but pangs of loneliness accompanied my memories. Aria had often repeated the instruction as I recovered to help me get through the pain, saying that it was her mother's remedy for calm whenever she was distressed. I hated that she saw me like that. My fear had emasculated me.

"It's okay, Declan. I'm here. I'm not going anywhere. Right now, all you have to do is breathe. Just look at me. I'll do it with you."

Memories were a place where both torture and treasures resided. Oblivious to everything by my renewed thoughts of her, I let out a long sigh. Aria's memory brought my breathing down to an average pace and delivered a brilliant light to the most recent dark terror. As I momentarily pacified myself by thinking of her, my bed began to jiggle.

"What are you doing here?" My voice broke the night's silence. I turned slowly toward the jubilant canine. Cody-girl shook the furniture with her tail wagging as she acknowledged her love for me. I leaned toward Cody, sinking my hands into her soft fur.

"You know she can't resist a man's touch." Carter made his way into my room. Rumpled and disheveled from sleep, he held two cups of coffee and handed one to me. "You look like hell. Another nightmare?"

I shrugged, diverting the question by continuing to pet Cody.

"You're drenched in sweat, Dec. Unless you had a hot dream, I'm going with the nightmare."

I glared at him. "Why do you have to go there, Carter? It pisses me off."

Carter shrugged. "So it was a nightmare."

My body language spoke volumes as my shoulders slumped. I shook my head to acknowledge the truth.

"Maybe you should talk to somebody about it."

I stiffened at his suggestion, the atmosphere shifting with my mood. "I'll figure it out."

"It's been months. Let's be honest here. I've poured you into bed more times than I like to remember and I've heard you yell her name in the middle of the night."

"It's the accident. In the dream, I'm always screaming for her to get out of the street." I handed the coffee back to Carter and held onto Cody for leverage to balance myself. The move didn't escape my brother's notice. He sat down across from me.

"No matter what you think, subconsciously you're trying to protect her."

I dropped my guard. "I must be. I still find myself yelling 'Go' to her and that's what wakes me up, the word *Go*. After that, I feel all kinds of pain."

He gave me an understanding look. "Maybe you should call her. If you hear for yourself that she's doing okay, maybe it will stop."

"She's better off without me."

"Who says, Dec? You?" Carter's raised eyebrow was a non-verbal challenge.

"Aria doesn't need me. I'm deadweight. She's young, beautiful, and smart. I'm a pain in my own ass most of the time with this." I directed his attention to my leg with a sweep of my hand.

"No, I don't think you really believe that," he disputed. "As far as being a pain in the ass? Yeah. You are that."

I ignored his attempt at a joke. "It's done, Carter. Like I said, she's better off."

"So what you're saying is that you don't love her?"

I kept my nose in the cup as my brother issued the challenge.

"Yeah. That's what I thought." He stood. "C'mon, Cody."

The dog followed my brother as he moved to exit the room, but before he did, he turned. "Ask yourself this—how are you going to feel when you see another guy with his hands on her?"

A flush of anger crept up my neck at the thought. I clenched my jaw and attempted to stay composed, but I was too tired to bullshit my brother.

"Yeah...again, that's what I thought." His tone was dark with sadness. "If that time comes, I hope you can hide your reaction from her better than you're doing right now."

Chapter 4

Aria

he stretch felt deliciously sinful as it relieved the tightness from my back and neck. As I concentrated on elongating and lengthening my body, I relished the new-found strength. Unfortunately, the focus that most people find when practicing yoga didn't help my attempts to purge Declan from my thoughts. Memory is such a tricky thing. If I smelled a familiar scent or heard a particular song, he came to mind. Even while doing the simplest task, like making a sandwich, I would suddenly wonder if Declan was eating or taking care of himself. But just as quickly as the thought appeared, so did my self-chastisement. I would tell myself that he didn't deserve my concern and that it was he who said that he was a "big boy and could take care of himself." It immediately removed any tenderhearted remnants I had toward him, but it was a daily battle. I swayed my thoughts away from him because I had other things to think about. I was going to see my mom.

My mother had moved closer to me after the accident. Although I had insisted that I was fine, my mom told me that she had nothing keeping her where she was. She has such a tender heart and she thought that Declan, Carter, and I could use her help. At the time, Declan and I were still in a relationship, albeit strained. Mom had jumped right in, making meals for Carter and me as we alternated going to the hospital to be with Declan. I had such tunnel vision. All

I could concentrate on was Declan, but I had overheard Mom and Carter discussing their helplessness at seeing the distance between Declan and me. I knew that she could hear my muffled cries during the night and it broke her heart. She had tried to engage me in conversation, but I insisted that things would get better. The last thing I wanted was to discuss Declan with my mother. He was so closed off and defensive and I wanted to hide how he treated me from everyone. His mood fluctuated regularly. Finally, something broke inside of me. I came home from the hospital that day and told my mother that my relationship with Declan was over and that if she continued to visit him, I didn't want to know the details. It wasn't until months later that she revealed that she had visited with him one last time and she wanted to share it with me.

"It's very hard for me to be here today, Declan."

Her tone was harsher than she had used before. Instantly, his guard went up and his response was firm. "I know what I'm doing, Jeannie. A year from now you'll thank me for cutting it off."

"No, I won't." She was the one who was firm now. "You think that I don't know what you're doing. I know exactly what you're thinking."

"I don't believe that you do. I love your daughter enough to make her hate me. You think this is easy for me? It's not, but she deserves better than a cripple!"

"What my daughter deserves is to make that decision for herself!" She took a step closer. "God knows why, but she still loves you. But I'm not surprised. She watched her father do the same thing to me. He was wrong, and so are you!"

"Aria doesn't know what's good for her…"

"Stop! Stop it right now!" Emotion cracked her voice. She took a deep breath and looked directly into his eyes. "Understand this— pushing her away is not loving her—but love can get you through this. You just don't have the guts to try."

She retrieved her purse and prepared to leave. Before she walked through the door, she turned and once again approached

Declan. It was evident by his body language that he was straining to keep his emotions in check. The expression on his face was pained, his spine was stiff, and his hands were balled into fists. In an unexpected move, she bent down and kissed the top of his head. As he looked up into her eyes, his own filled with tears that threatened to spill. "The way that you loved my daughter made me love you. You are an extraordinary man. One day you'll want her back because what the two of you have is special. What you need to decide is whether you are going to let the tough times pull you together or apart. I only hope that it isn't too late when you do."

As she turned to leave again, she felt Declan grip her hand. She looked back at him, but he had no words. Jeannie shook her head in sadness. "Fight hard to get her back. Fight very hard."

I wasn't sure what to think when Mom told me what had happened. I felt sorry for Declan and what he was going through, but I was also pissed off at him. He was the one who had brought Marisol into our house. I blamed him and he blamed me. It was a no-win situation. My mother tried to give advice, but I wouldn't listen. I didn't want her to interfere. Eventually, she had stopped giving her opinion.

Mom still wanted to stay nearby and I had agreed. I had gone with her when she was looking at houses. Mom wanted a place all on one floor that didn't need much work and was close to some of the local shops. It had been her lifelong dream to open her own flower shop and she deserved to have it. Most of her adult life had been spent taking care of my father and me. When we found the perfect home for her, a storefront nearby was also available for rent. Everything then fell into place and Mom realized her dream with the help of two investor friends. The shop was beautiful. She called it Sandy Ann's Flowers and Fudge to reflect the names of her investor best friends and her creations of cut flowers and arrangements, and an old family recipe for fudge. It was a hit! Who doesn't love a gift of chocolate and flowers? With some help and contact lists from Paige's real estate firm, as well as Katherine supplying the client list from The Studio and my company sending floral arrangements as a thank you to customers, she had quickly become successful.

Chapter 5

DECLAN

*S*ight could be deceptive and for a moment I hoped that my eyes were playing tricks on me. Unfortunately for my heart, that wasn't the case. My eyesight was quite reliable. As I left the restaurant after a lunch meeting, I saw her and my throat clenched. She didn't notice me because she was engaged in conversation. I didn't have to actually see Aria to know that she was near. The moment I stepped outside of the restaurant, I sensed her. No matter how much I have tried to tell myself that we will never be together again, Aria is as much a part of me as the blood in my veins. The distance between us is just a measure of space. There is no expanse large enough to separate us. Despite my best efforts, our connection is still strong. With every heartbeat, she is still in my blood; with every breath, she infuses life in me. Today wasn't the first time that I had seen her since the break-up and each time I do, I still feel the sucker-punch of loss. Her wild curls were piled atop her head and her beautiful blue eyes crinkled at the corners as she smiled. I savored the view.

Just as quickly as I saw her, she disappeared into a little shop. I looked up at the sign and realized that it was her mother's. I had heard that Jeannie Cole had opened a store called Sandy Ann's. For a moment, warm thoughts of Aria and Jeannie filled me. It instantly transformed to a hollow feeling in the pit of my stomach. The emptiness of not having them in my life wallops me. No matter how hard I try to convince myself otherwise, I ache for Aria—and I hate myself for it. I tore my eyes away from her mother's shop and walked to the car. Once inside, I sucked in a deep breath, then took two more.

Three deep breaths, Declan.

Dammit! Her voice filled my head. Even the simple act of breathing reminded me of her and how the sound of her instruction could soothe me. There was nothing I could do to escape it. Her words are seared in my mind every time I become overwhelmed and need to remind myself to breathe. Absentmindedly, I got into the car and closed the door. White rings formed around my knuckles as I held the steering wheel in a death grip. My attempt to relax my muscles was valiant, but ineffective. The smell of alcohol and leather comingled with the faint scent of nicotine as I noticed a pack of cigarettes in the console. Carter must have left them in the car. Although I had quit years ago, I needed something. Drinking had become my vice of choice after Aria and I had split up, but since I didn't have anything else available, these would have to do. I reached for one from the pack as I pressed the lighter into the console. I bit down on the filter before letting it dangle from my lips. As I pushed the hot coil to the end of the paper, I inhaled deeply. The smoke invaded my lungs and I closed my eyes, enjoying the heat. It was a momentary diversion, not enough to make me stop thinking of her.

I tossed the pack onto the passenger seat and leaned my head back against the headrest. Agony and ecstasy compete with equal force whenever I see Aria. I thought I had a handle on myself, but whenever she's around, I feel like a lovesick kid. The further I try to push her away from my mind, the more thoughts I have about her. Eventually, I'll have to face her. We have too many friends in common for us not to cross each other's paths. I don't relish the thought of that reunion. I was such a prick to her the last time I saw her. Nothing I say or do will erase that. An apology is in order at the very least. The backlash of emotions that occur whenever I picture that scenario are not pleasant. I deserve every negative thing she'll say and I have no doubt that she'll say plenty. Aria is a sweet and loving woman, but she's no doormat. She'll unleash the fury of hell on me.

The brief respite in the car gave me time to think without distraction and my memory strayed to the accident. I always travel down the same road of recollection every time I think about Aria. She is the reason that I got hit by that car and I remember that she ran because of Marisol. I also remember that we had discussed Marisol just hours before and I had assured Aria that nothing was going on. Why hadn't she believed me? *Because Marisol had her hands on your junk when Aria walked in, asshole.*

That image brought me back to reality. Over the past month or so, I'd been trying to understand the incident better. If Aria had actually seen Marisol grab me, then I needed to put myself in her place and see it through her eyes. If my grasp of the scene is correct and the situation was reversed, I would have killed the son-of-a-bitch that put his hands on her. That was the situation that I had trouble remembering: Aria and Marisol. I know that Aria had a grudge against Marisol because of me, but Marisol painted a different picture of our relationship. I don't know who or what to believe. Sometimes, the memories blur, fade, or congeal in various manners. I can't trust my memory and I'm still not sure about trusting Marisol. I don't remember why she was at my house that day. *Did I invite her as she says? Was I screwing her behind Aria's back? I know that Aria means more to me than Marisol, but was I lying to her then? Fuck! I hate this selective memory bullshit!*

Marisol is beautiful and she was kind to me during my recovery. The way that she told the story was that she and I were in a relationship and I was cheating on her with Aria. From the bits and pieces that I've been able to put together, it looked as if Marisol and I were together at some time and she had proof. She brought photographs to the hospital to jog my memory about us. The images showed us at clubs and at openings of restaurants and art exhibits. I traveled all over the world with her. My agent said that we worked and played together. In the photos, we looked happy. We were smiling and relaxed. No one has confirmed the feeling I have that we weren't as she says. When I asked my brother about it, he said that I never mentioned a relationship with her and he reminded me that the first woman I ever brought to meet the family was Aria. My friend Aimee is another person that I trust. We've been friends and colleagues for years. She, too, said that she doesn't know for sure about Marisol and me. I never confided in her who I was sleeping with. I know as sure as hell that I'm not celibate. Since Aria and I aren't communicating, the only information I have to go on are the stories Marisol told me and I don't believe all of them. My instinct tells me not to because I am a shallow and self-centered man. I'm too proud to rely on anyone but myself. If I'm going to get my life back, I have to remember things on my own.

What I never seem to war with are the mental pictures I enjoy of Aria. An image of her on the front porch fills the vision behind my closed eyes. She is wearing a flowy white top that settles on the top of her arms and she's flashing that infectious smile of hers. Her long dark curls swirl in the warm morning breeze and wrap possessively around her bare shoulders. I smile as I reminisce. I still believe that she's the most gorgeous woman in the world. She's pretty without trying to be. Aria without makeup is more beautiful than any woman that I can recall.

Vague images traveled through my mind as I remembered her not only in the morning, but sitting at the shoreline, walking barefoot in the sand, and in so many other poses. All are shattered fragments of memory. The events leading up to them and after them continue to escape me. What I know for sure is that she did—does—own a significant piece of my heart. It is reconfirmed every time I see her. The longing and desire to have her with me continue to intensify; I can no longer fight my best intentions to stay away from her. I told myself that I did the right thing by pushing her away, but my head was at war with my heart. Intellectually, I know that it's better for her if I stay away, but my heart is never going to believe it.

Chapter 6

DECLAN

"Hi there, boss. I have a few messages for you. How was your meeting?"

I hoped that my nonresponse indicated to my assistant that I wasn't in the mood to talk. After seeing Aria, I could feel another dark day looming heavy in the air. I tried not to discuss my personal life with Katherine. It isn't that I don't trust her confidence, it's because outside of the office Katherine is a friend to both Aria and me. I'll give her credit; she has remained a consummate professional through all of this and ensures that she doesn't step over the boundary between our work and personal lives.

As I looked at her face, I could tell that she was trying to gauge my mood. I know that I've become too mercurial for her liking. It's a wonder my personality change hasn't made her quit her job. More often than not, my demeanor is affected by physical pain; I've become a moody bastard. Cheerful feelings are a rarity and are usually displayed for the benefit of clients. Maintaining the facade is tiresome and Katherine often gets the wrong end of my tolerance. She may suffer, but the business doesn't. It's thriving.

"Declan? Did you hear me?"

I was lost in my dark thoughts and her hinted sarcasm agitated me. I spun on my heels. "What?" Her expression responded to my bark. Her brows, previously inquisitive, were now pulled together and completed a crestfallen look on her face. The immediate guilt pushed me toward an apology, yet none fell from my lips. "I heard you the first time."

She raised her arm from behind the desk, a handful of papers in her grasp. "Calls. For. You."

Her emphasized staccato words were deliberate and void of emotion. I walked toward her and took them from her hand. "Thank you." The mumbled words were said over my shoulder as I retreated into my office. I could tell that Katherine was pissed at me as her glare bore into my back like a dagger between the shoulder blades.

I threw my overcoat on the chair and walked to the credenza. My hands supported me as I flattened them against the oak. My head dropped from the weight of my thoughts. I shook it back and forth as I attempted to remove Aria's image from my mind. When I opened my eyes, the sight before me was Assawoman Bay. Aria chose this particular spot in the building for my workspace so that I could always enjoy the view. Even in my office sanctuary, I can't escape thoughts of her. And she was right; I do enjoy the view.

As my line of sight lowered, I spied the bottle. A snicker erupted as I was reminded that it, and the glasses, were a gift from her. The Baccarat crystal caught the light at certain times of the day, creating a rainbow reflection on the wall. I poured myself a bit of whiskey and stared at the tumbler in my hand. I was wound so tight that I felt like hurling it against the wall, but I couldn't bring myself to destroy something that she gave me. Instead, I sipped the contents, savoring the mixture of flavors. It was only a brief distraction, interrupted by Katherine's voice on the intercom. Instantly, I exorcised Aria from my thoughts.

"Your three o'clock appointment is here. Mr. Matthews and Ms. Franzi." Her tone was still flat, a clear sign of her irritation. It may have been because she can't stand Marisol, but it was probably because of me. Maybe a combination of both.

"I'll be with them in a minute." I bought myself a moment to check my reflection. Aria had designed a private restroom for me

24

within my office. I slipped inside the door, unl
smoothed and tucked in my shirt. I didn't like w
ror. My features had grown hard and were no
with youth or marketability. I splashed some wa
ran a comb through my hair. I hoped that a quic
wash would eradicate the whiskey's telltale smell   ...ʌcu off the
light and limped over to my chair; my leg muscles had begun to re-
bel. I slid open the desk drawer and popped the top off of the pre-
scription bottle. I tossed one of the pills into my mouth and swallowed it without water, then pushed the button on the handset's intercom. "Send them in."

When they walked through the door, I noticed the change of expression on Blake's face. It switched from pleasant to concerned.
Marisol didn't even look at me. Instead, she sauntered past me to the
other side of the room. Blake and I exchanged an amused look as she
commandeered the sofa with her coat and purse. "Make yourself
comfortable." Blake didn't miss the irony in my voice, but Marisol
was oblivious. Again, Blake and I looked at each other as he sat in
the chair in front of me. Marisol's cavalier attitude could be either
entertaining or irritating. At the moment, I couldn't decide which.

"How are you holding up?" Blake turned his back to Marisol,
ignoring her presence. "Summer is great here, but today it's cold as a
bitch!" He tilted his chin toward me. "I mean, how is your leg doing
in the cold?"

"It's fine," I answered, not wanting to get into a conversation
about my leg. Blake looked taken aback by my curt response, but he
got the hint to change the subject.

"Okay then," he said, the chill in his tone unmistakable. "Let's
get down to business. I want to talk to you about using part of your
building for Bella Matrix."

My interest was piqued. I leaned back. Though Blake and I had
enjoyed a close friendship in the past, I disconnected many personal
relationships after the accident, including this one. I had no desire to
mince words.

hat's in it for me?" My directness took him by surprise. The

eclan could make a business meeting seem like a visit with an

ld friend. No longer. I had no desire for easy banter or relaxed conversation. All I wanted was for him to get to the point so I could get drunk, but I wasn't fool enough to shut down an opportunity.

"A percentage of the business I generate through this location or rent. We could discuss it," Blake proposed.

"Twenty percent."

His eyes widened at my quick comeback.

"Ten," he countered.

"Fifteen and the deal's done today."

"Christ, Declan!" His stare was hard and his right hand gripped the chair arm. I displayed no emotion.

"What else would you need besides an office?"

"Not much. There's too much lag time between you scouting here and me seeing people in New York. If I'm here a few times a month, we can streamline the scheduling process. If it's okay with you, I can use Katherine to schedule appointments. I know that you are seeing people with potential, but if I can get Aimee to scout on my behalf, I can see twice the amount of people when I'm here. You know, time is money and all that."

Marisol suddenly found the conversation interesting. "What? Why Aimee? I know better than Aimee what kind of people the fashion industry wants and needs." Her indignant tone was unmistakable.

Blake turned in his chair, giving her his full attention. "Will you also be willing to help with paperwork, make photocopies, and record contact information?"

Distaste colored her expression. "That's secretarial work. I'm not interested. Aimee can do it." She raised the compact mirror in her hand and dabbed at her make-up, dismissing us.

Blake turned back to me with a gratified expression. "As we were saying..."

Marisol Chapter 7

*M*arisol had seen this look on Declan before. It was how she most preferred him—cold and empty. As she looked out the window and over the bay, she smiled inside at her luck. If she played her cards right, she could mold him into the perfect companion for her personal use by making him believe that she was his savior. His memories were confused and he was malleable. The plan had great potential.

Although her back was to Blake and Declan, she was paying attention to every word. She ran her palms over her skirt to smooth it and picked at something invisible on her sleeve. She couldn't wait for Blake to leave so that she could be alone with Declan. Though Blake might not notice, it didn't escape her that Declan had been drinking. His tone was hollow and his attitude was brusque. He rushed through the meeting, which appeared to have finished.

"Take care of yourself, Dec. I'll be in touch." Blake turned to her. "Are you ready?"

"No. I have a few things to talk to Declan about myself, then I will leave. Thank you. You may go." Her dismissive tone shocked Blake and the expression on his face proved it. She fought the tug at the corner of her mouth as he stalked toward the door. As Blake was leaving, he and Katherine crossed each other. Confused at his demeanor, Katherine looked from Marisol to Blake, trying to determine what had happened to cause the tension sparking the air. No explanation was offered, so she turned to Declan. "Here's the iced tea you requested." Katherine placed the glass on his desk.

"That was for me. Bring it here." Marisol's words fell on deaf ears as Katherine ignored her and left the room. Once she had Declan under her thumb, getting rid of the obstinate little secretary would add to her pleasure. "She's incompetent," Marisol said as she retrieved the glass.

"She's a good assistant," Declan defended.

"She couldn't work for me."

"She doesn't. She works for me."

Although Marisol meant her comment as a decree, Declan took it as a challenge. Marisol didn't want to argue with him; she had something else in mind. "You're a good man, Declan." Though tenderness wasn't her strength, she intended for the words to turn the conversation in her favor.

"Someone once told me that," he replied.

Marisol knew who that someone was and she didn't want him thinking about *her.* "Anyone can see that." She sounded a bit snippy, even to herself. She sweetened her tone to do damage control. "You poor thing. You look like you need a vacation."

Declan relaxed into his chair and lifted his leg up on the desk. As he sat back, his eyes closed. "I don't need a vacation. I was off work for too long."

"Don't be silly," Marisol chastised and came around to the back of his chair. "That wasn't a vacation. You worked hard to get well." She placed a hand on each of his shoulders and lightly massaged. She softened her voice. "You had The Studio on your mind and all of the details of this business the entire time you were recovering. No one knows that better than me. I see how hard all of this is on you. It's too much for one person to carry alone. You should let me help you."

Marisol's hands traveled down the front of him. She paused when she reached his chest and then moved a little lower to his stomach. The flesh was firm; the ripples in his abdomen were firmly felt beneath her fingers. She transferred herself to the side of him and as her hands continued the journey down to his thigh, his eyes opened. "You need someone to worry about you; your needs." She caressed and massaged until she reached her destination. She cupped his sac in her hand, rolling the tender flesh with her fingers. "No one knows better than I do that this business can be so...hard." She smiled to herself as he sucked in a breath. Her lips were mere inches from his. He was full and throbbing. He reached up and threaded his fingers through her hair. His eyes smoldered. She tried to lower her face to put her lips against his, but his fist tightened in her hair, holding her in place.

"What the fuck do you think you're doing?" His tone was low and harsh and his words were spoken through clenched teeth.

She swallowed. Though shaken inside, her composure remained calm. "I was trying to help you."

"I don't need your help."

His words were like a slap in the face. He let go of his grip as she pushed herself up. Her hand was still on his crotch for leverage and she felt him go limp. Once upright, she turned her back to him. "I'm sorry." Playing the injured victim, she dropped her chin to her chest. "I was trying to help, not make you angry."

"Keep your fucking hands to yourself and I won't get angry."

After a few moments of tense silence, she turned to him. "Declan, I know that men have needs. I want you to know that if you need me to...let's just say that it doesn't mean the same thing to me as it does to other women. It's just sex." She lowered her eyes until her lashes fluttered against the top of her cheeks. It was her best attempt at being demur. "Maybe not now, but the offer stands." As she peeked up, he raised his brows. His expression changed until he almost looked humored, so she smiled.

"Interesting offer, Marisol." He leaned forward on his desk and tented his fingers, the smile on his lips deceiving her. "Now, since we're done here, get your coat and get the fuck out of my office."

Chapter 8

Marisol

arisol sat at the edge of the seat and stared in the mirror. The game of cat and mouse that she had played with Declan earlier had marred her face with a line or two, but it would be worth it in the end. Inserting herself into Declan's life had taken more effort than expected. Though he denied the attraction, she was confident that, given time, she would get him into bed. Once that happened, taking over his business would be child's play. What should have been easy was proving to be difficult. While in the hospital, Declan was more impressionable. Now, he was skeptical of everything and everyone. She was extremely helpful to him while he had been recovering. Her performances had been worthy of an award. Digging deep inside herself, she had mustered a semblance of sweetness and tolerance. The hardest part of all was biting her tongue against his snapping attitude. Though he had rejected her sexual advance today, she was confident that he would eventually succumb to her.

Dealing with difficult men was such a chore, but Marisol had experience in that area. Her father was a cold, unforgiving man. Because of him, she learned at an early age how to hone manipulation skills. She was a master at forming superficial relationships. Once a connection was made, it was easy enough to fool people into thinking that she cared deeply for them. It was almost laughable how easily Declan had leaned on her when he had pushed Aria away. Both of them had disrespected her and both would pay for it, but the penalty for each would be different. She would use Declan and destroy Aria.

A rush of pleasure flooded Marisol at the thought of her plans for Aria. She was fragile. Declan had pushed Aria away and it had broken her. All that was left for Marisol to do was to finish what he had started. She hadn't solidified her plans for Aria, but there was no question that she would eliminate the threat. She had plans for Declan as well. He didn't know it yet, but one of Bella Matrix's biggest clients was planning a campaign for a new product. Marisol had slept with the client to ensure that Declan would be involved in the project. The shoot was to take place in Hawaii and the thought of having him all to herself in such a relaxing place pleased her. Of course Declan would be appreciative to her for requesting him and she would tell him how he could best show it. She wrapped her arms around her waist and hugged herself. She was a beautiful woman; he was a man with pent-up sexual frustration. This trip would be a splendid thing.

As Marisol lifted her eyes and looked into the mirror, she saw her reflection looking back at her. Her lips curled into a sneer. "What are you staring at?"

"*Nada.*" The whisper fell from the lips of her parallel image: her twin, Marchelle. "I wanted to let you know that I have finished what you asked of me, but I didn't want to disturb you."

Marisol's eyes narrowed as she turned to face her sister. "I didn't ask you to do it; I told you. You've done everything?"

"*Si.* Everything is in the trunk of your car. *Como usted lo pidió*—as you requested."

Marisol placed her hand against Marchelle's cheek and caressed it. She detested animals, but her sister was her favorite pet. "*Bueno.* You're a good girl." She paused for a moment. The similarities between the two of them always amazed her. Marchelle possessed the same beauty as Marisol, but they were different in every other way. Marchelle was sweet and did not view that trait as being a weakness.

Though they were identical in looks, sweet was something that no one could accuse Marisol of being. The back of her hand trailed down her sister's cheekbone before she withdrew it. They were so connected that she felt Marchelle's sadness as she removed her hand. Affection was a useful bartering tool for her sister's compliance, but one she used sparingly. *"Muy bonita Marchelle,"* she softly spoke. "You're such a beautiful girl." Marchelle smiled at the compliment. "Did anyone see you in the car?"

"No. You told me to be careful, so I was. I purchased with cash and placed everything in the trunk when I pulled into the garage. I made sure that no one was around, just like you said."

Marisol nodded her approval. "You're a good girl. Now you can make me some tea. When you bring it to me, I have some more things for you to do."

A sweet smile curved Marchelle's lips. "Of course, Marianna. Anything you want."

Marisol's hand struck her sister's cheek with a stinging slap. "I told you never to call me that. Marianna is dead and Marisol took her place."

"I'm sorry! I didn't mean it! It just slipped out." Marchelle's voice trembled and her eyes filled with tears.

"Marianna Valez has been dead for a very long time. Papi gave me that name and I don't want anything from him. Marisol is who feeds and clothes you! If not for her, you would be a plaything for some drug lord!"

Marchelle's face was full of remorse and she dropped her head to her chest. "I'm so sorry, Marisol. It won't happen again. I wasn't thinking."

"You'd better think, you little bitch, or I'll put you out on the street where the authorities will deport you!"

Marchelle's head snapped up. "Please. I won't do it again. I don't want to go back. I want to stay here with you."

The rapid rise and fall of Marisol's chest was equaled only by the angry flush on her skin. She struggled to calm herself. Threatening her sister was usually more than enough to keep her in line, but this time she had used physical force. She couldn't do that again. It had nothing to do with tenderness for her sister and everything to do with appearances. Marisol used Marchelle as a double when there was something she didn't want to do or people she wanted to distract. Putting marks or bruises on her would raise questions in the public eye—something she didn't need. After pacing for a few moments, she regained control and spoke in a more even tone. "Do I need to remind you of your purpose? How you earn your keep?"

"No." Marchelle's defeated tone satisfied Marisol, further diffusing her anger. She straightened her posture and raised her hands to her heated cheeks. Although she told herself that she cared nothing for her sister beyond what benefitted her, she felt a twinge of pity. Marchelle couldn't impersonate her very well if she acted frightened. No one would believe that of Marisol, so she moved to do damage control. She put her arms around her sister's shoulder and lifted her chin. "You know I'm not really angry with you," she cooed. "But I can't have you making mistakes. My safety is at risk."

Marchelle looked at her sister with cautious eyes as Marisol hugged her.

"I promise; I won't do it again."

"I've tried to do so much for you," Marisol chided.

"You have done so much for me. I love you for it." Tears trailed down Marchelle's face.

Marisol petted her sister's hair, as one would a soft kitten. "I am not angry with you anymore," she consoled. "It was a momentary lapse." She paused, moving onto her next thought. "Now, I have something else that needs your attention. We're going to Hawaii."

Chapter

Aria

9

The soft whirring of the white noise machine lulled me into subliminal ease. Like Pavlov's dog, visiting Doctor Sumner these past few months had preconditioned me to drop the guard I had so carefully built since my split with Declan. As soon as I passed through the office doors, my shoulders released their tension. I arrived early, but only by a few moments, because I found that too much time spent in the lobby challenged my focus and allowed my mind to dwell on thoughts of him. That particular train of thought was counterproductive to moving forward in my therapy sessions. At the same time, most of those sessions revealed how much I still care about him and how much I don't want to.

The click of the door handle interrupted my reflection and I felt my expression soften. Doctor Sumner appeared with a smile, her body language indicating that she was ready for me to come into her office. As I crossed the threshold, I headed for the overstuffed chair that I found most comfortable. It's so cliché to lie down on a couch in your therapist's office that the thought never crossed my mind to assume that posture. Although I've done this same thing many times, the first few minutes always seem slightly awkward. I nervously pulled my hair around and over one shoulder. I played with it to relax and remind myself that I'm fine. Anything I say here is safe.

Doctor Sumner peered over the top of her glasses and placed her notepad on her lap. She threaded the pencil through three of her fingers, then rested her hand on top. "How are you today, Aria?"

"Good." My obligatory response made her smile and she adjusted her glasses.

"Good to hear. Anything new?"

Now was my moment of truth. "Yes. I've seen Declan." Interest piqued, the doctor's brows raised. I steadied my voice and continued. "The fact is, that it wasn't the first time. I saw him twice—once over the holidays and another time."

"How did you feel about that?"

It was an inquiry that I had been preparing for, but I had no answer. My thoughts about Declan were constantly muddled. "I wish I could tell you," I answered and shrugged my shoulders. Exasperation with my dilemma was evidenced with a deep exhale. "I wanted to talk to him—just a chat—but I couldn't slow my thoughts down. I was happy to see him, but of course I couldn't say that."

"You didn't expect to feel happy?" the doctor inquired.

"I don't know. I've convinced myself that I could never feel something for someone who so carelessly disregarded my feelings." I shook my head as if the action would remove him. "I wasn't prepared for how I felt. My heart leaped into my throat like I was a kid in high school. The reaction made me second guess myself."

"You seem disappointed."

Her comment made me pause. *Was I?* I placed the heel of my palms over my eyes. "Hell, I don't know! I miss him, but don't think I should. Am I some kind of masochist? Like a dog who comes back to be petted after it's kicked?" I blew out a gust of air. "He hurt me—crushed me. What kind of sicko am I to still have feelings for him?" Removing my hands, I tried to gauge Doctor Sumner's reaction. She was good, keeping her voice monotone, but I thought I saw a hint of a frown.

"It isn't that simple, Aria. You were—and may still be—in love with him."

My eyes widened and my spine stiffened, but she continued.

"Let me finish. You've confided to me that you know that you've never been in love with anyone but Declan. Although your ending was messy, being with him had its 'up' moments. Until the accident, you thought that you would spend the rest of your life with him. You wouldn't be human if you didn't want to resolve this relationship."

"There is no way in hell..."

She put her hand up to stop me. "I'm not suggesting that you go back with him, but I'm also telling you not to rule it out. You have memories that he doesn't share."

"And therein lies my problem, doesn't it? The memories."

Doctor Sumner frowned at my self-deprecating tone. "The memories are a problem, yes, but those will be resolved. I believe that even if Declan doesn't try to remember, that the truth will reveal itself to him. You know that the good outweighs the bad and that is where we need to work. On your memories. When, and if, the time comes that the two of you talk, you need to have a handle on what is real—about your feelings, the accident, everything."

I slumped back into the chair. I hated revisiting all of this. But to move out of the stagnancy, I had to do it. I didn't have to like it. I peered up at Doctor Sumner. "So you don't think I'm a sicko?"

She countered. "Do you think you're a sicko?"

"I don't know." My voice faltered. I bit my lower lip as I thought for a moment, then I looked up at her again. "I have to find out if this thing with Declan is done or not."

"I believe we're dealing with two separate issues, Aria: your relationship with Declan and the accident itself. Your memories aren't different. They're too convoluted. One is tainted by the other." She rested her pencil atop the pad. Her expression softened. "I'd like to propose something to you. Something that, I believe, is a proactive exercise."

I arched my eyebrow. I couldn't remember Doctor Sumner ever sounding so cryptic. She smiled at me, the corners of her eyes crinkling softly. "Write."

"Write?" I echoed. "What good will that do?"

"I want you to write a letter to Declan. In fact, I want you to write several. It isn't for him, Aria. It's for you."

I laughed. The suggestion was ridiculous. Doctor Sumner had to be joking, except that she wasn't. The look on her face told me that she was dead serious. My neck straightened and my spine grew rigid. Every hair on my head prickled as my body responded to the bubbles of rebellion coursing through my blood. Irritation flushed my skin, uncomfortably warming me. I began to sweat at the very thought of sending a letter to Declan. *I'll be damned! Screw him! Screw her!* I looked her dead in the eye. She could stick this psychobabble bullshit because I was not pouring my heart out for him to walk all over it again. There was no way my resolve could be mistaken as I spoke my overly enunciated words through clenched teeth.

"Not. Happening!"

Chapter 10

CARTER

State government buildings held about as much warmth as an ice cube, but Carter Sinclair felt the heat of brotherhood as he walked through the Maryland State Trooper Headquarters. The officers were like family.

"Hey, Sinclair!" Sergeant Henry's booming voice yelled across the room. "What are you doing up here?"

The old man was a welcome sight. "I thought I'd come back and screw up your day!" Carter joked back at him. He made his way over to shake hands with his former superior officer. He looked around the room and noticed several vacant desks in the back. "Where is everybody?"

"They'll be filing in soon." Sergeant Henry turned toward the coffee machine and held up a stained cup. "Coffee?"

"Nah. I'll pass."

The sergeant poured himself a cup and went back to his desk. Carter had taken a seat in the chair beside it. The old man raised a bushy eyebrow. "Seriously, Sinclair. What's up? I thought you turned into a beach bum."

Carter crossed his leg, resting his ankle on his knee. "I did. I am, kind of. My brother can be a pain in the ass." His comment elicited a chuckle from the sergeant. "I figured we could both use a little breathing room, so I came home for a few days. I needed to check on the house anyway. Get my mail. The usual bullshit."

"I hear you." He nodded and then inquisitively narrowed one eye. "You been by the house yet?"

Carter's lips tightened into a thin line and he shifted uncomfortably. "Not yet."

Reading Carter's body language, the old man deflected. "How is your brother? The report said it was pretty bad. He got somebody saved, but hurt himself in the process?"

"It was pretty bad. The girl is safe—well, physically at least. As far as Declan goes, I don't think he'll ever be the same. Neither one of them will."

"Damn shame." The old man's lips turned in on themselves as he lowered his eyes and shook his head. "Sounds like a mess."

Carter nodded. "It's hard to watch him self-destruct. Lately, it seems he's been crawling into a bottle to self-medicate."

"Yeah, that's no good. You talk to him?" The sergeant inquired.

Carter leaned back and ran his hand through his hair. "I'm trying. I've talked to him and I've argued with him." He quirked an eyebrow and gave a little laugh. "Next thing I'm gonna do is kick his ass."

The old man cracked a smile, revealing nicotine stained teeth. "Now you're talking." He sat back and narrowed his eyes, suddenly more serious. "Have you thought about bringing him up here for a while? You know, mountain air clearing your head and all that shit."

"No." Sadness bled through his words. He offered no other comment.

The officer detected the sorrow still seeping through grief-induced cracks. It bothered him to see the pained weight still sitting on Carter's shoulders. "You know, Sinclair, what you're feeling is normal."

Carter's mouth quirked at the corner as he shrugged. "It's not the same. Nothing feels right. There's no light there with Lacey gone." Uncertainty filled his expression. "I did live there after she died. Before Declan got hurt."

"Yeah, but you didn't like it," Sergeant Henry quickly interjected.

Carter raised his head and grinned at the sly old fox. He never could hide anything from him. "No. I didn't." He took a breath. "Speaking of Lacey, I've been talking about having a gala in her honor."

The sergeant spit into his cup as he half choked and laughed.

"A gala? You? Christ almighty! You hang out with your uppity brother and now a party is a 'gay-la'."

Carter laughed too and gave him a look to knock the shit-eating grin off of his face. "Shut the hell up and listen, old man."

Still chuckling under his breath, Henry mocked him. He made the key locking the lips motion with his fingers, displaying an ornery streak that made his eyes twinkle.

"I've been talking about it with some of Declan's friends. They do this kind of stuff all the time for charities and the like. I want to start a scholarship fund in Lacey's name."

His curiosity piqued, the old man's expression sobered. Carter leaned forward and continued. "I don't know. I was just thinking about Lacey one night and how she enjoyed helping others. It was her nature to do nice things for people—something positive to help them. She loved kids, loved teaching, and loved being outdoors. I guess I thought if I could put something together that would make kids want to take school seriously and be active, that it would make her happy."

Sergeant Henry rose out of his chair and came around the desk. He sat on the edge and looked down at his former officer. "You're right. I think Lacey would like that. So whatever help you need? Let me know." He clapped Carter on the shoulder. "How can I help get this thing moving along?"

Carter readied himself to leave the barracks. It had been a good visit with his fellow troopers. As each one arrived for shift, the sergeant felt it was his duty to tell everyone about the benefit for Lacey. As expected, all offered support. He had said goodbye and was walking toward the stairway when Sergeant Henry's voice boomed.

"Sinclair!"

Carter's head snapped to attention.

"I need to talk to you before you leave." He motioned him over to his office.

"You forget something, Sarge?"

"Yeah," he answered, opening his desk drawer. "Have you spoken with Captain Jax since you left here?"

Carter shook his head.

"I didn't think so," Sergeant Henry said. "I figured you would have said something if you did." He held out a manila folder. Puzzled, Carter took it from his hand. "Seems the rental car company down on Main Street had a security camera. They think this is the person who was driving the car that hit Lacey."

Carter looked down at the grainy still. Shades of black, gray, and white were separated in minuscule amounts, but enough to form an image. He felt the blood leave his face as an invisible fist sucker-punched him.

"Jax wanted you to see it, Sinclair," Sergeant Henry said in an apologetic tone. "I know it isn't clear and it might be nothing. Their security camera is an old one.

Carter looked up, his eyes meeting the other man's. "It might not be clear, Sarge, but I think I know this person."

Chapter

11

DECLAN

O!

    I shot up in bed, my heart racing and my pulse pounding. I couldn't suck in enough breath. How could a simple word have such a profound effect? My memories had morphed into dreams. The twists and turns between fact and fiction distorted what I could remember. While dreaming, I could hear a female voice speaking so I deduced that Aria was done with me. Her edict indicated that she'd had enough. There was never a scene beyond the word, only feelings of helplessness and pain. The pictures that preceded it in my mind's eye blur until I can't figure out what's happening. I hate that I have no control over my thoughts and chastise myself for not being mentally disciplined. I have the same dream over and over. I had yet to make sense of it. I dropped my head into my hands. I'd formed a checklist in my mind that helped me to sort what I do know as fact. As always, the first moments of clarity aren't really clear at all. It was a terrifying feeling. The dream that was more a nightmare than peaceful rest continued to undermine the purpose of sleeping. The secure feeling that I used to have when I slept is gone. In its place is an oppressive pit of unconsciousness.

    "It's a dream. It's just a dream." I muttered to myself under my breath as I kneaded my forehead to ease an impending migraine. My hair was wet with sweat and the sheets were uncomfortably sticky.

As I calmed my breathing down to a normal pace, I tried to remind myself that whatever I was trying to remember might be best forgotten.

Just three deep breaths.

Her words reverberated in my ears as I swiveled my legs and sat on the side of the bed. I rolled my head from side to side, attempting to ease the tension in my neck. I had been able to attack everything else head on—the limp, the pain—but I couldn't stop the dreams from becoming nightmares. Whatever this shit was that had disarranged my subconscious had become my adversary. I hate how it takes over when I rest. It controls me and makes me its bitch. And I can't talk about it with anyone. I don't want to talk about it. A distant sound interrupted my thoughts. The usual ocean breezes had escalated to erratic gusts and the screen door at the kitchen creaked and banged against the doorframe. Carter would have latched it from the inside if he had been here, but he went back to Deep Creek to check on his house and he took Cody with him. It hadn't been this silent here in a long time and the stillness grated on my nerves. I am a man who likes being alone, but I don't like the feeling of loneliness. "It's too damn quiet," I heard myself say.

I walked into the bathroom and opened the door to the medicine cabinet. As I reached for my toothbrush, I saw Aria's sitting beside it. Even in little things she was still there. I squeezed a line of toothpaste and brushed my teeth. My reflection in the mirror looked like hell. I looked older and harder than I used to. I hadn't noticed the lines around my eyes before. Maybe that's because Aria had turned them into laugh lines. I closed my eyes and shook my head as if in doing so I could remove her image from my mind. I don't know why I tried. It was hopeless and I knew it. Once she got in there—into my thoughts—she rarely left until there was enough alcohol in me to drown her out. That was no longer working. I'd pass out and something about her was always mixed in with the nightmare. As I hung my head over the sink, I splashed cold water on my face. When I first came home from the hospital, I could easily dismiss thoughts of her because I concentrated on my therapy and getting the use of my leg to resemble something normal. Then I went back to work and I saw her everywhere—smiling, walking on the beach, wrapped in my arms. "No, no, no!" I smacked my forehead against the cabinet. I needed to give up. Aria was unique. Nothing I could do would ever make me stop thinking about her. "What the hell's wrong with me?"

I returned to the bedroom and pulled on a pair of sweatpants. My footsteps dragged down the hall and into the kitchen. Even making coffee wasn't without consequences, as this was the time of day that I loved spending with her the most. Her oversize soup mug/coffee cup sat beside the coffee maker. No Keurig for her. She said she liked the sound and smell of a regular one. Every corner contained a memory of her. As I leaned my elbows on the counter, I lowered my head. Wetness rolled down my face. People had surrounded me for months and noises, actions, and conversations had diverted my attention from the one truth that finally revealed itself. I'd been taken care of longer than I'd like to think. First Aria, then Carter. Today was the first morning I could recall that I was doing something that I used to overlook. Something that I used to do for Aria without thinking. It stirred something inside of me. Resentment, pain, and a warm feeling mixed with a dose of melancholy. It was what Oprah would call a "light bulb moment." They say that scent is a powerful aid in recollection and the pungent aroma of coffee exposed the truth to me. The fact that I tried to deny. A sob choked me as my voice trembled. I spoke the words that I had not said in months.

"I still love you."

Chapter

Aria

12

rite a letter. Doctor Sumner made it sound so simple. It wasn't as if Declan would ever see it. She said that it would give me a place for all of my unresolved feelings to go. I didn't know about that, but why not? Although I hadn't told her, a lot of strange things had happened. For instance, I would find myself crying when a song came on the radio. Memories would then surface. Where I was and who I was with when I first heard it. The answer was the same in every case. With Declan. As I made myself a cup of coffee, I pondered the idea a little more. Maybe Doctor Sumner was onto something with this writing purge. If I could get everything out, then I could move on.

I went over to the desk, coffee in hand. My prettiest stationery was in the middle drawer. I'd barely used it; instead, I sent texts and emails to my friends and family. But this letter was special. It was to him. And the stationery was so appropriate. I love pretty paper and he had bought it for me as a gift. It seemed only fitting to send it back to him with words that would tell him how I actually felt, at least figuratively. I took a deep breath. If Declan wasn't really going to receive it, I didn't have to hold anything back. I've never told anyone exactly what I thought of them. Maybe that was my problem. I made it too easy to hurt me. Like *I'm little Miss Sunshine and you can rain all you like on me.* I had always preferred to lift people up rather than tear them down. But no more. Now it was time to put away all the sweetness and let the bitter juices flow. To say exactly what I thought. Like my own personal coach, I talked up that line of thinking. I would be victorious when I no longer felt his hold on me. The hardest part was to put pencil to paper and just go with it. *I can do this!*

I set the cup on the chairside table and balanced the paper on top of a magazine. Pushing on the eraser end, I extended the lead in my pencil and began to write.

My Dearest Declan ~

"No. Too intimate and corny."

Declan.

"Too harsh and cold."

Dear Declan,
Days are long without you.

"Truth. Yeah, I'm going to tell him the truth."

Dear Declan,
I never thought I'd say this to you, but I miss you. Thoughts of you still occupy my mind, though mostly when it's quiet and I'm idle.

"Oh my God, that's so stiff. I'd never talk like that. Just the truth. Declan will never see it. Just get it out! Take three deep breaths and get on with it! Okay."

Dear Declan ~
I hate you. I miss you. I hate myself for missing you. Why did you have to make me feel the things I do? Nobody loves me like you

do. Nobody thrills me like you do. Nobody gets me; nobody killed me like you. I guess I should thank you for showing me what love was, but I died inside when you pushed me away. I hope you did too. What you don't know, is that because of my dad, I understand. He thought he was doing my mom a favor, and maybe you think you were doing the same. Dad didn't want to be a burden to Mom, so he pushed her away. I'm going to tell you what I didn't have the guts to say to him; you're wrong. When did I give over the right for you to make my decisions for me, or did you just take it? I haven't figured that one out. I felt so guilty about the accident, but you were equally as wrong. You let Marisol come between us. Then you broke my heart. And I let you. After loving you, I don't know if I'll ever love again. I'm not sure if I want to or if I can. I've come to the conclusion that the only real love I'll ever experience is the one we shared. If I'm either brave enough or stupid enough to let someone else into my life, I'll never give to them what I freely gave to you. Because I'm broken. And you're to blame. If that day ever comes, and you see me with another man, I hope you suffer. I hope that it kills you to see me with someone else knowing that it could have been you. I would have shared my life with you, but you took away my choice. Just know that when he's kissing me, I'll be imagining your lips. When he touches me, I'll moan for you. I'll hear your voice inside my head. And you won't be able to claim any of it. Because you're the bastard who made it this way by throwing me away. I was the best thing that ever happened to you. You and I both know it. And in spite of all the bull-shit, I'm the fool. Because, as much as I hate it, I will always be,
    Your Aria

I laid the pencil down. I blinked away tears as I felt the weight from a layer of bitterness fall away. It was numbing. I curled up into the chair, my body forming a ball, and let fresh tears fall.

I looked at the clock. Half an hour had passed. The rush of tears emptied me and the silence in my head was the first peace I'd had in a while. Somehow expelling the words did make me feel better and I thought differently about the exercise. If one letter could help, maybe more would cleanse me completely. Nothing had changed with Declan and nothing would. Only my outlook. Even if I couldn't stop loving Declan, exorcising my thoughts of him would make the void so much more bearable. It could work. Suddenly this assignment didn't seem so crazy and I began to think that the exercise had merit. It was safe and I didn't have to weigh my words to make my feelings palatable. I could say whatever I wanted because no one would get hurt. My prince was a frog and I got to tell him all about the warts he'd caused. I called him out on all the ugliness and pain. I was able to tell him that I think he's a piece of shit. That there isn't a snowball's chance in hell that he will ever get me back. That he doesn't deserve me. That he's a shallow bastard. And he can rot in hell for all I care.

Chapter 13

Marisol smoothed her skirt in the mirror, appreciating how the designer had fitted the material to her hips and ass to accentuate them. Reaching for her Balenciaga bag, she checked her reflection to see the completed ensemble. She straightened her posture and brushed her hand along her cheekbone and up into her hair. Pleased with her image, she was confident that she was as close to perfection as a person could be. The knowledge made her smile. She turned as light footsteps fell behind her, alerting her to her sister's presence. She peered out of the window as she addressed Marchelle, never bothering to look at her twin.

"Is the car in the garage?"

"*Si.* When I finished getting everything on your list, I stopped at the gas station. It has a full tank and is clean. Just the way you like it."

Marchelle, ever the loving one of the two, looked down at the carpet. Marisol appreciated the act of submission. She walked over to her sister and stroked her hair to confirm to the woman that her services were appreciated. Her twin's devotion incited feelings of both endearment and disgust, but Marisol was determined to use Marchelle's weakness to her advantage. After all, she'd been doing it for years. The dynamic between the twins had originated in childhood. Marchelle was the weaker of the two; Marisol was stronger.

She had always protected her sister against the older siblings and children that threatened to hurt her. She even protected her against the biggest bully of them all: their father. "Good girl," she said as she removed her hand. "I want you to launder and put everything away while I'm gone. I'm going to see my attorney. I expect you to finish before I return. Understand?"

Marchelle nodded, a look of satisfaction crossing her face. She knew that it was an honor for Marisol to trust her with such expensive things. "You're beautiful, *mi hermana*."

Marisol smiled, once again turning toward her reflection. She gently ran her fingers over her face, stroking her flawless skin. "Indeed, I am."

Mr. Dietz's appearance neither thrilled nor excited Marisol, but his purpose wasn't to attract. She needed his legal expertise. Nothing about him was attractive. He was shorter than her preferred height in men and he had less hair than she found acceptable. His style of business attire couldn't be called a style at all. What she did find acceptable was his undeniable attraction to her. In fact, she expected it. He greeted her with an outstretched hand. "It's a pleasure to meet you, Ms. Franzi." He invited her to sit with a wave, then took a seat behind the desk. "When you indicated on the phone that you were in need of an attorney, I honestly expected that you would prefer one based in New York."

"Well, Mr. Dietz," she cooed in her familiar style, "I need someone local and you have come highly recommended." His chest puffed out as pride inflated his lungs. Marisol leaned over just enough to assure the man had a good view before she continued. "I wish to venture into the area of real estate ownership. I've been spending more time in this beautiful location and I find that purchases here could provide a good return on my investments."

Not wanting to mislead a client, especially one of Ms. Franzi's caliber, Mr. Dietz felt it only fair to give full disclosure. "Ms. Franzi, I can help with the contracts, but I work with a real estate company for all other facets. They will be happy to assist you with any repairs on the properties, as well as take care of renting them for you. Is that acceptable?"

"Of course," she said, humoring him. "I've given the undertaking much thought. What I need for you to do is to set up a corporation for me. An umbrella under which to place all of my properties, as I'm thinking of purchasing more than one." She leaned into his desk and smiled seductively.

"Ms. Franzi, are you sure that a beautiful woman like yourself wants to be bothered being a landlord?"

She scoffed at his words. If it weren't for the fact that time was of the essence, she would have dismissed him for his condescending comment. Men never thought that a woman with beauty could also have brains. "Why, yes. I know exactly what I'm doing, Mr. Dietz," she said with all the charm that she could muster, speaking slowly and succinctly. It was imperative that she make herself clear. If he still showed any signs of hesitation once she finished, she would take her business elsewhere. "Specifically, I would like for you to form a corporation for me. I would like to employ Davis Realty to procure and manage the properties and Cole Construction to do any needed repairs. I would like to use those two companies exclusively. You will obtain a dossier of available properties, which you will give to me for selection. Once I have made my choices, I will authorize you to make the purchases on my behalf. All of this you will run through my corporation, which no one will know that I own. Do I make myself clear?"

Mr. Dietz was dumbfounded. It was apparent that he had underestimated her as just another pretty face. He nodded, indicating that he understood.

"As I am proposing nothing illegal, I don't foresee any problems. Would you agree?"

51

Again, he nodded. Flustered, he searched his desk for a pen. Having found it, he looked up with intent. "And the name of said corporation?"

Finally! The plan was in motion. It was only a matter of time before her goals would be achieved and she could realize her plans for Aria and Declan. She pressed her lips together as a smile curved them. Marisol had given great thought to the name. One that she had chosen as an alias. Its mention would one day define her. Her name and the name of her company would synonymously define beauty and brains. She raised one eyebrow and gave Mr. Dietz a sly look.

"Vencedor."

Aria Chapter 14

I arrived early to Doctor Sumner's office, anxious to tell her how much better I felt. I attributed it to the letter writing. Although I still had little clarity on certain aspects of the accident, it seemed that the more letters I wrote, the better I felt. Because of this, my desire to move forward in therapy was increasing. My primary goal was to push through my recollections. I wanted to put them in order. To rationalize what had happened. I was having difficulty with the scenes in my head. They didn't match up with my intuition. Something was missing. A piece of the puzzle that would complete the picture. I was no longer torturing myself because my constant introspection assured me that I wasn't the cause of Declan's injury. In my dreams, I strangled my screams. Something prompted me to shout, but it escaped me. It was a regular nightmare. My throat would constrict and I would speak his name in a whisper instead of a shout. My guilt was in a state of limbo within my subconscious and I all too frequently imprisoned myself there. However, my imprisoned emotions began to dissipate as I wrote the letters to Declan. My words grew bolder with each new one, and my attitude followed suit. Today I planned to tell Doctor Sumner that I was ready to take the next step, to explore more adventurous forms of therapy to expose the truth of what had happened on Coastal Highway. The root of my distress was waiting to be found. It was locked away in my subconscious, but I wanted to set it free. I wanted possession of my thoughts, not the anxiety that had cast an ugly shadow over my mind. Now that I had faced my emotions regarding Declan, it was time to face whatever darkness my memories had tucked away. One thing I could never deny—Declan had earned my heart; I hadn't given it away. I was grateful that falling in love with him had grown me into a passionate woman, and painful or not, I would never regret loving him. It made me happy to realize that I was a survivor and my character was strengthened because of my experiences. I entered Doctor Sumner's office and settled in the comfortable chair. Our routine continued with the usual question and answer.

"How are you, Aria?"

"I'm good. How are you?"

I watched as Doctor Sumner relaxed into her chair and smiled over the rim of her glasses. "You're quite smiley today. Anything you care to share?"

I tucked my leg beneath me and leaned into the thick pillow at the back of the chair. "You gave me good advice and I followed it." Doctor Sumner's raised eyebrow elicited an unexpected giggle. "I've begun the letters. I've written several."

Pleasure registered on the doctor's face. "That's great! And it's helping?"

I dipped my chin as tender thoughts crossed my mind. "Yes. It's been working well. Knowing that he'll never see the letters has made me very free with my words. I've poured my heart out to him in those letters." I looked at her matter-of-factly. "At first, it was awkward. I didn't think I could do it, but then I wrote the first one. I started it a couple of times. After a few tries, it was like my heart cracked open, you know?"

The doctor nodded, affirming that she understood. Tenderness filled her expression. She motioned for me to continue, so I did.

"Although at first, the emotions overwhelmed me, but once they began to come out I filled a sheet of paper. I cried. It felt right to tell Declan exactly how I felt with no reservations. When I finished, I crumbled the paper into a ball and chucked it in the trashcan."

The doctor sat up, impressed, as she tapped her pen against her chin. "I'm curious. You said more than one?"

"Oh my gosh!" I laughed. "I've written about nine or ten! In two of them, I was so pissed off at him that when I crumbled it up, I stamped on it, ground my heel into it, and kicked it across the room!"

The doctor belly laughed. "I'm sure that made you feel better.

"It did!" I confirmed. "Then I danced on one of the letters while I sang Aretha Franklin's *Think*! Who would have known that something so simple could make me feel so much better?"

Doctor Sumner's brows inched up and she gave me an *I-told-you-so* look.

"Okay, you would," I acknowledged.

"I'm glad that it's working for you and that you're progressing."

I shrugged my shoulders, slightly reluctant to tell the doctor the other news. "I am, but…"

"There's more?" the doctor queried.

"Yes. I want you to hypnotize me."

"Excuse me?" Doctor Sumner fought to contain her surprise.

"Can't you do that? Can't you make me remember the details by hypnotizing me?" I heard the trace of desperation in my voice. I wanted to piece together what had happened and she was my best chance at doing that.

"If that's what you want, I think there's a better option."

I was eager to hear more and leaned forward in my seat. Doctor Sumner removed her glasses and put them in her lap. "There's a treatment used with people suffering from Post-Traumatic Stress Disorder or PTSD. It's called EMDR therapy—Eye Movement Desensitization and Reprocessing. It can be an effective form of treatment. Once we identify the most vivid visual images that you remember of the accident, we can try to unlock them. Maybe identify something positive as well as negative. Think about it. I can give you some information.

I stood. I wrapped my arms around my waist and walked over to the window. Everything that I could see through the glass was transparent. The colors outside of the panes were so vibrant. There was no distortion. The scene was crystal clear, exactly how I wanted my memories to be. I straightened my spine and squared my shoulders, turning toward Doctor Sumner. "Let's start now."

She looked at me for a moment, trying to gauge my confidence. Once satisfied, she continued. "I'm not certain how much we would accomplish today because we've used so much of your time already."

"I have time left. I want to start," I said as I looked at my watch.

"We won't get the full effect, but we can try." Her open hand extended an invitation for me to sit, so I did. "Relax. I'm going to hold up my finger and I want you to follow it with just your eyes. Don't move your head, okay?"

I nodded.

"I want you to talk about the accident. Start at the beginning if you can, but if there is a particular scene that jumps out at you, we can start there. Where would you like to begin?"

"When I crossed the street and looked back at Declan."

Chapter 15

DECLAN

The throbbing in my leg began around the same time every day. The pain was a constant reminder of the accident and everything that had happened as a result. Especially the loss. I relied on whiskey and sometimes combined it with medication. I knew it was dangerous. Without Carter around to play nursemaid, I would have to face my truth; I was risking myself to addiction. Day after day, I tried to eviscerate the internal and external heaviness. There were many facts that I needed to face and most of them stemmed from questions I asked myself. The most significant: *What was more difficult to lose? The love of a lifetime or the use of a limb?*

The first truth that I needed to face was the state of my leg. Although it doesn't work as well as it used to, it hasn't affected my career as much as I had anticipated. My features have grown stern and the industry has become increasingly open-minded. More physically impaired models are breaching the perfection barrier. The popularity of several military veteran amputees has proven that there is a market for people as they are and not the perfection that the industry would have you believe. I have been approached about photo shoots, but turned them down because I thought the offers were out of pity. I'm thankful that times are changing. It's good for me and good for The Studio, so I may do photo shoots again. And once I get my shit together, I might be able to get Aria back. When I close my eyes, I'm afforded the luxury of seeing her and being with her. I can't fight myself any longer. I want her. I need her.

As time passed, I could see that Marisol was feeding me lies throughout my recovery. At first, I believed her, but the more I healed, the more things became clear. I didn't let on to her that now I know that most of what she's told me about my past are lies. I couldn't help but wonder what her end game is. *What's her plan?* When I first discovered her deception, I thought that she might be after money. Then I dismissed the thought. She has enough of her own. That can't be it. Then I thought it might be The Studio, but why would she want it? She acts like everything inconveniences her, so I can't picture her wanting the responsibility that comes with owning a business. I was at a loss. There was something that I was missing. Something that I had to see before it bit me in the ass. I popped two breath mints into my mouth. Even though I was easing off of the whiskey, I hadn't stopped completely. I still found it necessary to hide the smell of alcohol on my breath. I ate them just in time, because someone was walking into my office. "You couldn't knock?" I grinned as Carter walked in.

"I missed you too," he chided. He took a seat in front of me, a serious expression on his face. "You got a few minutes? I need to talk to you about something."

Carter asked very little of me, but gave so much. His tone was sober, which made me equally so. "What's up?"

He leaned back in the chair and sucked in a breath. Concern was etched on his face as he ran a hand through his hair. "I want to do something in Lacey's memory. I'm going to need your help because you're much better at this shit than I am."

"Why?" I had to admit that I hadn't thought about Lacey's death since I had become so self-absorbed.

The lines around his eyes and mouth softened. "To keep Lacey alive? To make something good out of something bad? Because I think she'd want me to? Take your pick."

"What's the goal?"

"A scholarship. In her name. Maybe two: academic and athletic. I guess it will depend on how much I can raise."

It was apparent that he had thought this out. He might not have known how to carry it to fruition and that's why he was telling me. I have experience. I've put on fundraisers for my charities. I could do this for my brother. In some small way, I could give back. The thought made me feel better. "What can I do to help?"

He sat up, apparently blindsided that I agreed without an attitude. I had been a bastard to him and guilt washed over me. I had to atone for my behavior because Carter didn't deserve how I had treated him. The thought surfaced that maybe this was where I could start—by being a decent person to my brother.

"I'd like to use your place if that's okay."

"Not a problem. What else?"

"Katherine and Aimee have been helping me put together ideas. Can you spare them for a couple of hours or days? They said that they would help if it was okay with you."

"That's fine, Carter." I smiled. He was so out of his element that he was unnerved. Something I'd never seen. He had always been my reliable, steel-nerved older brother. He was a rock for my mom when Dad left and was a substitute father for me. I'd always been able to talk to him about anything and he had always had the answers. Who would guess that something social would be his Achilles' heel? "Whatever you need to pull this off, you have my support. I think it's an excellent idea."

"Thanks." A pregnant pause passed between us and his mouth tightened into a thin line.

"Something else?" I prompted.

"Yeah," he nodded. "I want to invite Aria."

Chapter 16

DECLAN

I didn't expect that my stomach would drop to the floor, but that's what happened at the prospect of interacting with Aria. It was inevitable that we would be in the same company at some point. Why not for something like this? "That's fine with me."

"Really?" Carter's eyes widened.

"Yeah," I nodded. "I mean, let's face it; Aria would want to be there. I think she'd be offended if you didn't invite her."

"That's what I figured," he answered.

"I'll suck it up. It'll be fine." The resignation in my voice was unmistakable. "Aria adored Lacey. She was brokenhearted when she died. She should be there."

I could tell by the look on Carter's face that he wondered what had happened while he was away. The truth was that I'd had an attitude adjustment. Since he was the closest to me, he was the first one that was owed an apology for how I had been behaving. "Carter, I want to say I'm sorry." His eyes clouded with suspicion at my words, but it was imperative that I convey the message. "I've been acting like a dick. Or a spoiled brat. Take your pick, but I'm moving forward. I can't keep having a pity party." He was skeptical, I could tell. "Okay then. What brought all this about? I go away for a couple of days and when I come back, it's like you took some kind of nice pill."

"Something like that." I got up from the desk and walked around the room. My leg had grown stiff and I needed to stretch it. I could feel Carter's eyes on me. "As far as Aria goes, I think it's better for everybody if the first time we interact it's for something positive."

Neither of us spoke for a few minutes, then Carter changed the subject. "I went to the barracks while I was up in the mountains. It seems Captain Jax has a lead in Lacey's case."

"No shit?" I was shocked and surprised. The investigation had been stagnant.

"Yeah, I know," Carter said. "I felt the same way when I heard, but they showed me a picture of the person who rented the car that they think hit Lacey. It isn't the best quality, but it's the first real lead."

"So they know who it is?"

"No. Thing is, I think I know who it is."

"That's great!" I interject. "If you know who they are, you can arrest them."

"I wish it was as easy as that. They can't arrest someone just because I recognize them. There has to be evidence." He stood and dug in his pocket, pulling out a piece of paper. He unfolded it and held it out to me. "Take a look."

"How can you tell anything from this?" The picture was hard to make out.

"Look again," Carter encouraged. "Take your time. Who do you see?"

I did as he asked, focusing and moving the paper back and forth in front of me. Like on one of those drawings that has a hidden image, my eyes began to register the picture within the picture. I felt sick as the truth slapped me in the face. "Shit!"

"Yeah," Carter nodded.

"What the fuck?" My eyes widened. "It can't be. She wasn't in Deep Creek then."

"Yes, she was. She came up to me at the cemetery."

Shock and anger fought for equal time as emotions unleashed like a storm inside of me. "How the hell did I not know this? You didn't think to say anything to me?"

"What are you talking about, Dec? I didn't even know who she was. She told me she was a friend of yours!"

I calmed myself. "Why the hell would she be in Deep Creek? Except for me, she doesn't know anyone there." As I aligned my thoughts, realization emerged. "She was following me!"

"I was pissed at you, don't you remember? You were smothering me. I told you to take Aria back to the house. She approached me after you left. She said she was a friend of yours and offered her condolences."

"Damn it, Carter! Why didn't you tell me?" My mind raced. I checked off the possible reasons that would explain why Marisol would go to Deep Creek. Other than her bullshit explanation of offering sympathy, the only reason was to mess with me.

"I didn't think it was relevant. And it wasn't. Until now." He stood, a murderous look on his face.

"I'm sorry." Anger filled me.

"If it was her, I think that she was stalking you. After everything you've told me, and how she acted at the hospital, I believe she didn't want you with Aria. That's the only reason I can come up with." His hypothesis had merit. "If she knew you were coming up to my house, she might have followed you just to be a bitch. There's no logic to crimes of passion."

"Crimes of passion? There was no fucking passion." I gave him an incredulous look. "I was never involved with Marisol. If she thinks so, it's in her mind."

"Whatever the reason, Dec, the mountain roads are tricky. All I can think is that she rented a car to follow you and hit Lacey."

"She'd have to be one cold-hearted bitch not to dial 911."

Sadness shadowed his face. "Yeah, she would."

I softened my voice. My brother's pain was palpable. "I can't imagine how you feel."

There was an uncomfortable vulnerability in my brother's posture. His battle for composure was evident and he wasn't alone. I wanted vengeance for my brother and Lacey. If Marisol was guilty of murdering Lacey, she was toying with my brother and me. As I thought of how she dripped sugary sweetness on both of us when I was in the hospital, all the while knowing that she took something precious away from us, I was incensed. I walked over to Carter and clapped my hands on his shoulders. We were an arm's length apart. He looked at me with disgust in his eyes. There was something I could do; I could help him. My tone was full of determination and my spine was rigid with resolve. "If she's guilty? Let's prove it. Let's get the bitch!"

Chapter 17

DECLAN

I returned to my office after walking Carter out, my thoughts muddled. The combination of Carter's revelation, my emotions, and the alcohol that I'd ingested earlier was wreaking havoc with my stomach. I felt like I couldn't trust anything anymore: my memories, my so-called friends, or my judgment. It was going to be difficult to play along with Marisol as if everything was fine.

The days that followed were challenging. It was all I could do to be near Marisol without bellowing accusations at her. On one such occasion, I sat silently when she made herself comfortable in my office. She brought magazines, newspaper clippings, and cards from friends which she read aloud, just as she did when I was in the hospital. She told me how much she cared about me and I fought to keep the food in my stomach. I downed two whiskeys while in her presence—one for believing her lies and one for being a fool. I tried to decipher what was fact and what was fiction. In the meantime, my memories were becoming clearer and I didn't like what they revealed.

I had spent more time with Carter lately, listening rather than talking. He told a very different version of my life than Marisol did. He talked to me about things that he had previously dismissed. Things that Lacey had said about her conversations with Aria. Carter explained that he had not betrayed Lacey's confidence sooner because he thought it was just girl talk. He now thought differently. Carter said that Marisol had tried to insert herself between Aria and me. The more he told me, the more my recollections blended with the truth. I was no longer wavering as to who I believed. Carter wouldn't lie to me. The most difficult challenges for me now were pretending with Marisol and thinking of ways to right my wrongs.

Although we were still in the process of gathering evidence, the case against Marisol was growing stronger. I had to ensure that her trust in me did not waver, which was proving to be harder than I thought. My efforts to decrease my alcohol consumption were in vain because the more time I spent in Marisol's company, the more I felt like drinking. I would look at her and all I could see was Lacey—alone, broken, and suffering on the road—and it just about crushed me. If that wasn't enough to drive me to the bottle, the sight of my brother's silent torture also twisted my insides. The only bright spot for both of us was planning for the upcoming benefit in Lacey's honor.

Marisol had spent more time in my office today than normal. She had some plan for bringing kids over from Colombia like foreign exchange students for The Studio. After she left, I wanted to go home and shower. Her brand of filth left a residue that I couldn't wait to wash off; even though I knew that I should stay and sleep a little bit of the drunk away, I didn't want to. I stumbled to my car as the rain began to fall. The only thought running through my head was of how Marisol had played me. She continued to think that I was buying in to her bullshit. I wanted to be the one responsible for her conviction. I wanted to lock her ass up and throw away the key. But it still wouldn't wash away my guilt from hurting so many people. I wrapped my fingers around the steering wheel as my eyes misted with tears I couldn't shed. I didn't deserve my own pity, much less anyone else's. I was not a victim. I had known what kind of person Marisol is, yet I didn't protect the people I love from her. I'm no better than her. The rain came down harder. The drops reverberated as they pinged on the roof. Sheets of water fell upon the windshield and the wiper blades did little to slice through the downpour. Just as the rain had graduated from gently falling into a raging storm, so did the anger inside of me. My thoughts snarled with chaotic intent and they swirled inside my head. I loathed my former self-absorption. How could anyone forgive the part I'd played in their pain? I didn't deserve forgiveness. I grinded my teeth and pressed on the gas. My accomplishments were nothing in comparison to how I'd failed. I was barely concentrating as the highway rose and rushed before me. My fingers flexed as my vision blurred. The storm was violent and all hell was breaking loose. The car careened out of control as I slammed my foot on the brake. I spun wildly as the vehicle fishtailed. Anger switched to panic as I fought the steering wheel. In a matter of seconds that seemed more like hours, I wrestled with tons of metal as I swerved on the drowning blacktop.

Finally, the car stopped.

I gasped for breath. The only sound that I could hear was the slap of the wipers against the windshield. I was shaking violently and the rest of my body reacted. My knees knocked, my hands trembled, and my left eye twitched. I wanted to take my hands off of the steering wheel; I had to peel each finger away. I tried to regain my bearings, but my body was reacting in slow motion. During the mayhem, the car had conked out and I realized that I was not sure about which position I was facing on the highway. I turned on the ignition and restarted the car. I was too shaken to drive home, so I pulled off to the side of the road.

As I looked out across the street, I saw a familiar neon sign. A rumble began deep in my belly and made its way up my chest to my throat. The irony of my location wasn't lost on me. I was at the place where I needed to be. The place where I would begin my reconciliation. I saw Aria's mom through the shop window and I exited the car. The water dripped off of me, puddling around my feet as I walked toward the door. The sign said *Welcome*, but I wasn't sure that sentiment applied to me. Although fate had led me here, I didn't suffer delusions of Jeannie welcoming me with open arms. Why would she tolerate me when I had behaved so badly? She had shown me nothing but kindness and I had repaid her by treating her daughter like shit. Apprehension immobilized me as I stood outside looking in. The building had Aria's signature on it and I smiled as I took in her handiwork. Everything she touched she made beautiful. My house, her mother's shop, but most of all, me. She made me a better man. I had to make this right. Pride be damned.

 Chapter

DECLAN

18

I gathered my nerve and pushed the door open. The tinkling of a bell chimed as I walked in. A warm feeling wrapped around me like a blanket as I inhaled the fragrances of chocolate and flowers. A shadow appeared in my peripheral vision. As I turned toward it, I saw Jeannie staring at me. Although I stood more than a foot taller than Jeannie, fear raised the hairs on the back of my neck. For a moment, I wondered if she would kick me out. I wouldn't blame her if she did. Our eyes locked. Seconds passed that felt like an hour. I couldn't muster anything to say. All I could do was swallow the lump in my throat. She gave me a harsh look and clasped her hands at her waist.

"I wondered if you'd ever come to see me." Her voice was soft but convicting.

"If you don't want to talk to me, I can go."

A flash of pity showed in her eyes as she sensed my hesitation. "To be honest, I have mixed emotions."

I took a deep breath. "I don't expect anything, Jeannie. Well, nothing other than honesty."

"Damn it, Declan! You hurt the person I love the most in this world. I can't be more honest than that!"

My head fell in shame. I didn't know how to react. I just stood there.

"You hurt her and because of that I want to hurt you." She took in a deep breath and let out a sigh. "I loved you because she loved you. The hell you put her through…"

"I know, Jeannie." My confession momentarily halted the conversation. I looked down at the floor, embarrassed. Jeannie took a few steps closer to me and placed her hand on my arm. I looked at her.

"I guess you went through hell, too."

I nodded. Jeannie's expression softened. "I know that to say I'm sorry isn't enough, but right now it's all I have."

She scoffed at my statement. "Your apology isn't what I want; I don't really know what I want. You did such a good job at tearing my daughter down that it took months for her to bounce back. How could you do that? I know that you were in pain, but how could you take it out on Aria? You meant everything to her. I wasn't sure I would ever get my daughter back! Do you know how that feels?"

I could hear the anger in Jeannie's voice. Though I wanted to make her understand, I wasn't sure I could explain myself. I swayed. A funny feeling washed over me and I felt dizzy. The room swam before my eyes and my leg trembled. It didn't escape Jeannie's notice and she rushed to steady me. "I'm all right." My harsh tone stilled her, but only for a moment. I softened my voice. "I'm sorry. I'm not used to this. It's still hard for me to accept help from anyone."

She pulled a chair out as she held onto my arm. "Sit." She walked to the door and flipped the *Open* sign to *Closed*. "There was a reason you came here today."

"I want to tell you my side—if that's even possible—but please, give me some time before you speak to Aria."

Jeannie hesitated, giving me a wary look, but then her posture relaxed. "I'll hear you out and I'll keep your confidence."

"First, I want you to know that hurting Aria was never my intent. Just the opposite." It was a start and Jeannie listened with interest over the course of the next hour. I had nothing to gain by being dishonest, so I told her everything. Every fear, every intention, and every heartache. I took in her reactions. As she fought to stay composed, my heart broke. I saw the conflict in her expression more than once as I purged myself of every action and reaction that I could remember. When I finished, Jeannie said nothing.

Her eyes misted as she looked into mine. Then she reached over and took my hand into hers. Her voice was barely a whisper. "I believe you."

Aria Chapter *19*

*P*aige and Aimee had arrived at my house and were waiting for me. The three of us had plans for dinner and Aimee was growing impatient to leave. "What's taking you so long?"

I stuck my head out of the bathroom door, a flat-iron in my hand. Aimee shook her head disapprovingly. She didn't like anyone inconveniencing her. "Why are you doing that?" Exasperation laced her tone. "It's still raining. Your hair's going to be all frizzy by the time we get to the car."

I ducked back into the bathroom, ignoring her. "I want to wear it straight. Stop giving me a hard time."

She waved her hand, dismissing me. While she was busy concentrating on what I was doing, Paige had walked into the adjoining bedroom. I watched them both through the reflection in the mirror. Paige took a seat at the antique vanity and gingerly removed her make-up case from her purse. Aimee looked at Paige and then at me, her body language chastising both of us. "Really? Both of you now?" She let out a huff. "Fine! Do what you've got to do. I'm checking your fridge. You two are hopeless."

As Aimee walked away, Paige gave her an eye roll. "Just think of us as your helpmates," she quipped. "We're delaying your dinner to help you keep that skinny-ass model figure."

"Yeah, right!" Aimee's voice faded as the distance from us grew.

I looked over at Paige. "You're mean," I accused.

"Sure I am. And she's the one who gets paid to look cute." Paige turned to me as I unplugged the flat iron. "I'm ready when you are. I just like to give her a hard time."

I crossed the room and peeked over her shoulder into the mirror. "Give her some pity. We can eat dessert. She can watch."

A few minutes later, our final touches complete, Paige and I approached the kitchen. Apparently, we startled Aimee. She was hunched over the trash can. She jumped as I came up behind her. The can was one of those flip-top kinds that you operate by putting your foot down on a pedal. As she heard me approach, she jumped. The top clanged as it snapped closed. Aimee quickly turned around, guilt written all over her face.

Paige grinned smugly. "What has you so jumpy?"

"Nothing." Aimee removed her hands from her pockets and brushed over them with her palms. I could only guess that she had taken a candy bar from my hidden stash.

"Something," I interjected. "Stuffing in a few empty calories?" Her back straightened and she tossed me an indignant look.

"None of your business." Aimee walked into the living room, retrieved her purse, and slung it onto her shoulder. She straightened up and walked past me toward the front door. Paige and I exchanged looks, then followed behind her.

We had demolished our pasta and were moving on to dessert. I held a menu out to Aimee. She put her hands out in front of her. "No."

I jutted out my bottom lip. "Life's too short; have dessert."

Aimee shook her head. "I can't. Really. I shouldn't have eaten that pasta."

"Please! You didn't have half as much as I did," Paige countered.

"And I'll have to work off every bite. You want dessert? Have dessert."

Watching Paige and Aimee's bickering was like looking at a verbal tennis match. Aimee served a comment; Paige answered back. Volleys back and forth of jokes, snide remarks, and statements of fact seemed to happen every time the three of us got together. I stared into space as our server approached. "Ladies, can I get you some dessert?"

"No!" All three of us answered at the same time and a little harsher than we should have. The poor kid was taken aback by our abruptness.

"Sorry," I apologized. "We'll just take the check." He nodded and walked away from the table. I shot Aimee and Paige a look. "Do you think you could tone it down a little?"

"I'm sorry," Aimee apologized. "I have a shoot coming up soon. We'll be in bathing suits and every ounce shows on camera."

"I couldn't do what you do," Paige said. "I like food too much."

Aimee shrugged. "You don't know how challenging it is. You indulge a little here and there and before you know it, you're not getting work anymore." She looked away. "I don't expect you to understand."

Paige's expression grew repentant. She looked over at me and gave a little shrug.

"I understand," I soothed. "Remember? I used to live with a guy who was calorie-phobic. We were only kidding." I took a sip of my iced tea as the minor tension faded. "So where are you going? Where's the photo shoot?"

Aimee's expression brightened instantly. "Hawaii!" She made a little hula motion with her hands.

Paige leaned back in the booth. "I'm jealous. I hate winter. Love the beach, but hate the cold."

"Why don't you both go with me?" Aimee's eyes widened, excitement lighting her face.

Paige and I exchanged glances. "What?" Paige said. "We can't just go to work with you. Can we?" The question was hopeful.

"Yes, you can! I want you to!" Aimee answered, suddenly perky. "We'd have so much fun! We only shoot during the day, so we can hang out together at night."

"And your clients would be okay with that?" Paige asked.

"You won't be at work with me. While I'm at the shoot, you can go shopping. We'll do things when I finish for the day. C'mon."

"I don't know…" Hesitancy shrouded my happy thoughts. If Aimee was going to work in Hawaii and because Declan often worked with her, that meant that Declan could be…

"Stop it, Aria!" Aimee interrupted my train of thought. "I know what's going on in your head and you have to stop. I never know where he's going to be. I haven't worked with him in months, so there's a good chance that he isn't going to be there."

"But there is a chance that he will be."

"So what? Are you going to avoid every place that he could be? Besides, we didn't do anything for your birthday. Wouldn't you want to celebrate it somewhere tropical?"

One thing about Aimee—her attitude was infectious. It was cold and I had never been to Hawaii. The thought of sun, shopping, and Mai Tais held promise. Besides, I had been much too serious of late. Both Paige and Aimee waited for my response, anticipation glowing in their eyes. My mouth inched up in a grin and I rendered my decision. "Does Aloha mean *hello* or *goodbye*?"

Chapter 20

Declan

I fumbled in my pocket for my phone. When I pulled it out, I saw that it was Carter. "Where'd you go? I expected to see you two hours ago."

I hit the button on the phone display to put it on speaker and continued in the direction of where I had left my car. My clothes were wet and cumbersome, but the conversation with Jeannie made me feel like I'd removed fifty pounds. "You wouldn't believe me if I told you, but I'll fill you in when I get home." After unlocking the car, I got inside and started the engine. "I'm going to stop and get us some food. When I get there, we need to talk."

"That sounds cryptic. What happened?"

"Nothing...yet. I have an idea and I want to run it by you." I was certain that I was only adding to his bewilderment but what I had in mind was better discussed in person. "I'll tell you this; I think it will serve both our purposes."

I caught Carter tossing the top of his beer bottle in the trash as I walked through the door. His brows arched as he sniffed the air. "Are those cheesesteak subs I smell? I thought you said you didn't eat that shit."

I tossed the bag onto the table. "Tonight I have an appetite." Looking from the bag to his face, I noticed his pleased expression. "Stop eyeing it up like a vulture and grab some plates." I went into the guest bedroom to get something dry to wear. I hadn't slept in the master since Aria left. Carter had filled the drawers with my things thinking it would be easier for me to get around on the bottom floor and he was right. If I ever go back upstairs it will be to take Aria into my bed.

I heard the hinge squeak on the cabinet door as Carter opened it to get the dishes out. "Well, hell!" His tone dripped with sarcasm. "It must have been one helluva day. When was the last time you ate one of these? When you were fifteen?"

I ignored the question. "I went to see Jeannie Cole tonight." Since there was no other noise in the house, I heard him cough. Apparently, that news was making him choke on his drink.

"Damn, Declan! Did she rip you a new asshole?" He shouted the question.

I grabbed a dry t-shirt from the dresser drawer and pulled it over my head. "I'm sure you would've liked that," I scolded as I walked back into the kitchen.

"She'd be justified," he returned. "You did treat her daughter like shit."

I pulled out a chair across from him and stretched out my leg. It ached from a combination of slamming on the brake and the weather. It didn't escape my brother's notice.

"Leg giving you trouble?" Concern filled his voice.

I shrugged it off. "It's the weather. It's more of a pain in the ass when it rains."

Carter nodded in understanding and got up from his seat to go to the refrigerator. He removed another bottle of beer and set it in front of me on the table. "So what's up?"

I twisted off the top and pulled a long drink. Thinking back on the events of the day, I realized how much of a turning point the past few hours had been. I had escaped death twice: once when the car was spinning and secondly since Jeannie didn't shoot me dead upon sight. I placed the bottle back down on the table and returned my attention to him. "Like I said, I went to see Jeannie. We had a long talk, and yes, she somewhat ripped me a new asshole. She also forgave me—a little bit." I grinned. It would take time, but I planned to earn Jeannie's and Aria's forgiveness.

Carter smirked. "You're a lucky son-of-a-bitch. I would have bet money that she'd have slapped you."

"Yeah, well, I was completely honest with her. I told her some stuff that I haven't even told you. Beyond the suspicion we have about Marisol's involvement with Lacey's accident, the things that she's been telling me aren't jiving with what I remember."

Carter tipped his head in my direction. "You're remembering more? That's a good thing, I think."

"I didn't want to say anything, but I have been remembering, and ever since you told me about your suspicions, I've given more thought to the stuff Marisol's been saying. I think most of it is bullshit. My memories of my life before the accident are getting pretty clear. The details don't fall in line with what she's been telling me. I know she's been lying."

"Lying? Marisol?" he mocked. "Let me ask you something; why didn't you talk to me more when you lived in New York? I'm your brother."

"I don't know. Before Aria, I was a closed book. I don't think I shared much about my life in New York with anybody. It was all me. I was a self-absorbed, hard-headed prick, and you have my permission to kick me in the ass—but not today. Between talking to you and Jeannie, and me piecing a bunch of shit together, I feel like I need to be in a psych ward!"

Carter laughed, the sound escaping his chest with his words. "Yeah, right!"

I humored him. "What's so funny?"

He scoffed. "As if I need permission to kick your ass."

Now I was the one amused. "Yeah, you think that, okay?" I

pulled my ankle up on my knee and rubbed my calf. "Bullshit aside, I do want to talk to you about this thing with Marisol."

My brother's posture tensed and his fingers tightened around the neck of the bottle. "I told you; Captain Jax is investigating further. He wants to show the picture around. See if she stayed in any of the hotels or bed and breakfasts. As much as I hate it, we just have to wait and see what he comes up with."

"I think I can do better than that." Carter looked at me with interest and I took a swallow of my beer.

"You can't jeopardize the investigation, Declan. I won't let you." The warning in his voice was evident.

I shook my head as I leaned forward. "I won't," I assured him. "But what if I can lull her into a false sense of security? If I give her what she wants, she might let her guard down and hang herself."

He gave me a wary look. "And what does she want?"

I sat back in my chair, my emotions a mix of resignation and determination. It was the first time in a long time that I thought that I could accomplish something for the people I care about. I had to try for Carter and Aria. Sacrificial lamb or not, it was the only way to get to the truth. I looked him straight in the eye.

"Me."

Chapter 21

Aria

"Are you ready to begin?"

It was the same question I'd been asked for months and I didn't feel like I was getting anywhere. I'd been having such a good time with my friends since the last time I saw Doctor Sumner that I had entertained the thought of canceling this appointment. The reason I didn't was because I realized that it was time to get back to work. If I had any hope of clearing my mind before the trip to Hawaii, I would need to dig deep. The question that Doctor Sumner just posed had more possible answers than she could imagine. I was willing to start fresh on so many levels—to remember what happened that day, move forward from it, and heal in spite of it.

At each session, the doctor spends ten minutes setting me at ease. I like the EMDR therapy. It's not only helpful, but also fascinating; although it took me awhile to get the hang of it, it seems to work. While we are discussing a particular event, Doctor Sumner stops moving her finger and it's as if my brain freezes on whatever image is in my mind. If it is irrelevant, we move on; but if it is painful, we discuss it. Once resolved, we dismiss it and move forward. My only disappointment so far is the fact that I've remembered nothing useful about the accident.

"I'm ready." Since the mental and physical comfort of the patient are key to the success of this type of treatment, I tuck my feet beneath me in the chair. I'm hopeful that one day I will remember everything. Maybe today would be the day that my psyche would cooperate and stop playing tricks on me.

"Okay, Aria, in our last session we had gotten to a point in your memory where you were running from Declan toward the street. Follow my finger as I recant what you've told me, okay?" I nodded and she began to move her finger from left to right as I focused. "You were running from him because you were hurt and angry," the doctor added.

"Yes, I was. When I walk into the house, I see Marisol with her hands all over him and I snap. I'm jealous and he had never given me a reason to feel that way before. Something comes over me and I run. I wasn't running away from him; I just didn't know what else to do."

"Good; where did you run to?"

"I don't know," I answered, still following the movement of her finger. "There was no particular destination because I wasn't thinking. The hurt was overwhelming."

Doctor Sumner ceased moving her hand. "Now what do you see?"

I looked up in the air. There was a transparent projection screen in my mind's eye. "I'm on the street."

"Are you in danger?"

"No."

Doctor Sumner wrote something down as my attention returned to her. "Let's continue."

Once again, I followed her finger as she spoke. "You're in the street. Declan is behind you."

"Yes. I hear Declan's voice. It has a different sound to it. I've never heard it quite like that before. It's almost urgent—the words are forceful, but fearful—if that makes any sense. I'm trying to listen to the warning in his voice."

"What do you do?"

Her inquiry moved my memories further. "I'm on the street and I step backward. I step up onto the curb. Declan's shouting. He wants me to get out of the street. When I look over I see him—and Marisol."

"Stop," Doctor Sumner directed.

"Oh my God!" I blurted out the words. My heart raced. There was a band tightening around my chest and I began to hyperventilate.

The doctor reached across and touched my hand. "Calm down. Whatever you see, it can't hurt you."

I couldn't look at her, but I gripped her hand. I felt like I was sinking and she was my only lifeline. The image was trapped, unmoving in the center of my mind. I pulled my feet out from under me and planted them on the floor. I was spinning and I tried to anchor myself to the ground by grinding my soles into the carpet. No matter what words Doctor Sumner uttered, there was nothing that would remove the image as it branded itself to the forefront of my consciousness.

"Aria, look at me," she commanded.

I couldn't. I didn't.

"Aria...Look. At. Me!" She had never raised her voice to me before, so the demanding tone pulled me from my distress.

I felt the sting of tears as they filled my eyes; my lips trembled as I attempted to explain. "I saw it." I had no voice and my words carried on a whisper.

"Saw what, Aria?" Doctor Sumner gently probed.

There was no working through it. I couldn't un-see it. Not this time. The doctor continued speaking, trying to console me as tears fell from my cheeks onto my lap.

"You have to tell me. It's not talking about it that's been hurting you. Do you understand? Let me help you."

I was hesitant to say the words aloud for fear that their truth would crush me. "He was trying to help—trying to get to me. Then I saw it. I saw everything. And I couldn't help him. I couldn't help.

81

He didn't even scream." Tears flooded my eyes as I gulped back sobs that wracked my body. Heartache crushed me; mine and Declan's.

Doctor Sumner patted my hand, her voice soft and reassuring. "What you saw was terrible. Seeing someone you love hurt, especially when you can't stop it, takes a terrible toll on a person. You can't undo it and you wouldn't be human if seeing it didn't move you."

I shake my head. "No, no…you don't understand."

"What don't I understand? If you tell me, we'll sort it out together."

I looked up at her face. How could she help me to sort out something that made no sense? I should have left well enough alone; left everything buried deep where I didn't know it and it couldn't hurt me. Instead, my new nightmares would forever shackle me with the truth that I had hoped would set me free.

"I remember."

Chapter 22

"Marchelle! Where are my bathing suits?!"

Marisol's voice traveled through the condominium as she tore through the clothes in her closet. The swimwear she sought was especially sexy. Although her question began as a simple inquiry, her impatient nature turned the task into a full-blown garment interrogation. She could barely find anything since she had tossed every item she had touched onto the floor. No matter. She would have Marchelle organize and put everything away. Again. For the third time that week.

Marchelle came running from the other room and retrieved one of the suitcases resting against the wall. She gripped the handle and wheeled it over to Marisol. "*Toda está en la bolsa*," she said, holding it out in front of her.

"Use your English!" Marisol scolded. "How do you expect me to use you if you can't say the simplest things? At some point, we will switch places. I can't have your behavior raising suspicion."

"*Si*...um, okay." Marchelle gave her an innocent look.

Marisol glanced at the suitcase; scorn washed over her face. "Oh my God, what did you do? Pack? I didn't tell you to do that." Her irritation was evident. She unzipped the hard shell case and rummaged through the contents.

Marchelle approached her and knelt down. "May I help you?"

She reached for an item that was tossed aside, but Marisol slapped her hands away.

"No! You can't help me! You could have helped before, but you didn't. These aren't the things I want to take on the trip. I'm trying to find the white bathing suit with the cut-out back." Marisol's tirade was interrupted by the ringing of her cell phone. She flung the handful of clothes in Marchelle's face. "Find it for me!"

Marchelle began to dig through the pile, but was nudged forward by the sting of Marisol's hand hitting the back of her head. "Not the bathing suit, you idiot! The cell phone!" Marchelle dropped the clothing and proceeded to search the room.

"My purse, Marchelle! My cell phone is in my bag!" Marisol stomped over to the table behind the sofa. Finding her purse, she held it in the air and shook it back and forth. "Right here!" She pulled out the cell phone. Although it had stopped ringing a moment ago, it was ringing again. She waved her hand over the disarray as she moved into another room for privacy. "Get this stuff up now!"

As Marchelle hurried to gather an armful of clothing, Marisol's voice changed from bitter to sweet for the person on the other end of the line. "Hello."

Marchelle welcomed the momentary reprieve from her sister's anger. She moved everything to one side of the room and was folding and placing each article of clothing into a neat pile. After a few moments, she heard the telltale sign of Marisol's return as her high heels clicked against the floor.

"That was Blake's assistant at Bella Matrix. It seems that I have not been requested to go to Hawaii, which is very odd to me. I know this client well and I've been the only woman in his advertising campaigns for years." She looked down at her sister. "This news doesn't make me happy." As Marchelle watched with interest, Marisol paced the room, talking to herself. "So they have everyone they need for Hawaii? I don't think so!" Determination rose within her and she looked back at her sister who was still scrambling to make order of the mess. "I had plans for Hawaii. It was my one opportunity to get Declan away from here." She was lost in thought for a moment and then her chin popped up. A smile crept onto her lips and she once again turned her attention to Marchelle. "They think they're so smart, but they don't know me." Marchelle stopped her actions and gave Marisol a puzzled look. Marisol tilted her head as she smirked at her sister. "I may not be going for work, but I'm still going to Hawaii."

Aria Chapter 23

My thoughts began to lighten the moment I was able to stare out the window of the plane. After eleven hours, the cloud wisps had faded my concerns; once we disembarked, a bronzed beauty with waist-length black hair approached. I bowed my head, gracefully accepting her gift of a flower lei which she slid onto my neck. She smiled, her soft voice a caress to my ears. "Aloha."

"Aloha." I repeated the greeting. Holding the flowers within my fingers, I inhaled deeply. The fragrance further intoxicated me with the island's calming effects. The decompressing sensations from the short time I had been in Hawaii assaulted my senses of sight, sound, and smell in the most delicious way. I was at the mercy of a powerful native spirit and as it wrapped around me with a comforting warmth, I found it easy to let my concerns fall away. I was determined to have an enjoyable vacation.

As much as Aimee's personality is different from mine, it was great that she was so pushy as to demand that Paige and I make the trip. Although I was hesitant at first, this was one more step in my recovery. I love Declan. I will always love him. I hate what he did to us, but I've learned that I can hate what he did and still love him. These are facts that I must live with. Although he would never be aware of my feelings, and thus, they wouldn't be reciprocated, I've learned that I am a survivor. Life goes on and I'm adapting. When Aimee suggested the vacation, she had said that it wouldn't be the same without me. She also asked me if I liked myself enough to have fun. Guilt. Emotional blackmail. She had used some dirty tricks to convince me to come. And I'm so glad she did.

A car was sent to get Paige and me from the airport. The drive proved to be even more stunning than the brief introduction to Hawaii's beauty that we encountered at the airport. The colors burst in brilliant hues everywhere I looked. My view from the car window showed bright flowers, every shade more dazzling than anything I had ever seen before. Black volcanic rock against crystal blue ocean waves nearly screamed for attention as white foam washed over it. Chickens and roosters walked freely about, parading almost obscene vibrancies of oranges, reds, golds, and browns. I had never noticed that there was so much color in the world. Everything and everyone seemed so alive here.

"Look at our hotel, Aria." Paige interrupted my thoughts. "It's stunning!" She pointed her finger toward The Grand Wailea.

As we entered the lobby, our royal treatment began. Tropical drinks that blazed with appeal and color were placed in our hands as we were taken to our suite. The bellman opened the door, launching us into the lifestyle of the rich and famous.

"Dear Lord! All of this is for us?" Paige gasped as she took in the scope of our accommodations. Luxury and opulence resonated within the walls, transporting us to another world. We watched as the bellman walked down the hall to place our luggage in our respective rooms. Then he left the suite. Silence filled the space. We both looked around to ensure that we were alone. Then, we turned to each other, stared for a moment, and squealed like little girls.

"Oh my gosh! This room is crazy beautiful!" I turned around and took in everything once again.

"I know!" Paige sounded almost giddy. She traveled from room to room, commenting on each, before coming back to the living room. "This place is huge!"

The smiles on our faces said more than words ever could. "What?" Paige looked over at me, her expression inquisitive.

"Nothing. It's just that you look like a kid on Christmas Day!" I felt the same way and expected that my expression was a mirror image of hers. I was simply stating the obvious.

"Of course I do!" she replied. "Have you ever stayed in a hotel like this? No, don't answer that! I've known you forever and I know you haven't. How does Aimee stay grounded?"

"I guess if you do something enough, you just get used to it.

Paige shot me a sarcastic look. "Really. I'm not kidding here. Aimee hangs out with us all the time and she just seems so...normal. If this was the kind of life I had, I'm not sure that it wouldn't go to my head."

The clicking sound of the door handle alerted us to her arrival. "What go to whose head?" Aimee walked in on the conversation.

"Girl! You've got some crazy stuff you've been hiding from us," Paige said as she jumped off the sofa to hug her. "This place is an eleven on the one-to-ten scale. Do you stay at places like this all the time when you're working?"

"Oh, this little place?" Aimee remarked with a laugh.

Warm memories filled me as I recalled the many times I had gone with Declan when he was working. Although the size of this suite was larger than anywhere we had stayed, they had been equally as beautiful. I couldn't help but wonder how it would have felt to have been in Hawaii with him and a feeling of longing for him and the way we used to be washed through me. I was distracted as Paige's and Aimee's voices brought me back to their conversation.

"The agency and the clients treat us well." Aimee went into the kitchen and took a chilled bottle of wine from the fridge. She placed an appetizing tray of fresh fruit, cheese, and crudités on the granite counter. We followed behind her and each took a glass as Aimee filled them. She held hers up. "To friends."

The tinkling sound of crystal wafted in the air as Paige and I touched our glasses to Aimee's and returned the sentiment. "To friends."

Chapter 24

DECLAN

*D*iscovering the most secluded spot possible on the beach, I unbuttoned the top few buttons of my shirt and took a seat. As I pushed my feet under the sand, I felt the cold more on one foot than the other. It was a blatant reminder of the nerve damage; but unlike before, I was no longer angry because of the loss of sensation. My continued sessions with Doctor Rhodes were proving productive. I was more in control of my emotions and my thoughts were clearer. With each day that passed, I was becoming more like my old self. Although the accident had produced irrevocable changes, it was necessary for me to return to the man that Aria fell in love with in order to win her back.

The island breeze blew the stiff cotton shirt and it fluttered back and forth against my skin. The Pacific wind had produced a pleasant day on the Isle and I was glad that I had decided to make the trip. Aimee and Jonatan had convinced me to do this shoot, and as Jonatan had wielded his camera, his constant comments were reassuring. He never pulled any bullshit with me to spare my feelings; in fact, the opposite was true. His references to my upper body being "cut" and "buff" had boosted my confidence that I still had a physique that was marketable. Those words and the beautiful setting had done so much to lift my initial apprehension and the beauty of Hawaii was working its magic on me.

I watched the metamorphosis of colors in the Hawaiian sky. It could almost be a spectator sport for people with a need to relax. In only two days, the concerns that suffocated my daily life were blown away by the warm winds. The waterfall shades in the clouds streaked the sky as sunset approached. Bluish hues attracted me the most. I compared them with my memory of Aria's eyes. The recollections were haunting. She was my motivation to clean up my act. I wanted to be the man she had fallen in love with. I had cut way back on the drinking, only enjoying an occasional beer with my brother. Although no one could accuse me of being a boy scout, I was making progress. A confirmation had come by way of having lunch with Aria's mom. The invitation had been her way of checking up on me, but it was a welcome diversion. She had said that I was "looking good" and would be "a good catch." I smiled to myself because I agreed with her. I had a few unresolved matters, namely cornering Marisol to find out about her involvement in Lacey's death and getting more work, but there was only one person that mattered in the end.

Aria.

I continued to watch the sky until all of the clouds turned to a dark black blue. As I walked back to the cottage, I encountered what seemed like a million stars. They distracted me to the point that I almost didn't hear a noise in the house when I closed the door. It couldn't be Carter. He had just texted me to tell me that he was going to get us some beer and would be back soon.

Survival instincts kicked in and I glided around the doorway to the kitchen. As silently as I could, I pulled on the cutlery drawer to open it. After grabbing one of the steak knives, I fisted the handle and walked down the hallway. The sounds were isolated to one of the bedrooms. Apparently, some asshole thought that my brother and I were easy marks. I heard a heavy thud. I focused on the shadow of footsteps that moved beneath the door. I leaned back against the wall as blood rushed in my ears. The pace of my heartbeat nearly doubled. Whoever the bastard was, he wasn't worried about getting caught. As I placed my hand on the doorknob, it occurred to me that I should have just backed out of the suite and called Security. My only advantage was the element of surprise.

"AHHHHHHHHH!"

The sound was a battle cry. I raised my hand, the knife firmly in my grip. I made ready to stab anywhere I could reach. Whoever it was, I didn't want to kill him. I just wanted to maim him enough to incapacitate him. Instead of rushing toward me, the violator retreated so quickly that he fell back, banging his head against the wall. His hands came up and he clutched his chest.

"Declan! What the hell are you doing?" Eyes wide open, Blake's shocked expression met my startled one.

"What the hell are you doing here?" The two of us stared at each other as we both caught our breath.

"That's not the greeting I was expecting!" He nodded toward the knife in my hand. I looked down. My knuckles were white from the force of my grip. I looked back at Blake. He had slid down the wall and was sitting on the floor, shaking his head in disbelief. I pointed the blade down toward the floor just as I heard Carter come up behind me.

"What the...?" His words trailed off as he took in the scene. A shit-eating grin filled the lower half of his face. "When you boys are done playing, you can join me for a beer."

As Carter walked away, I extended my hand out to Blake. I pulled him up; once he was standing, he brushed off the front of his shirt and pants. "You could have killed me, you know."

I dismissed the dramatic tone in his statement. "Yeah, but I didn't. Again, what are you doing here?"

His expression transformed from indignant to amused as he snorted at me. "You should ask your brother."

Aria Chapter 25

While Aimee worked, Paige and I went shopping. Aimee had told us to get something to wear to a party. Paige and I didn't need an excuse to shop. We had such a good time picking out a few things to wear that the day flew by. As we entered our suite, we saw that the dining area had been beautifully set. No paper plates or red solo cups in this place. The table was dressed with crystal, china, and a fresh floral arrangement. Delicious aromas competed for our attention as a chef readied our meal in the kitchen. "Hell-ooo," I said in a singsong fashion.

Our chef looked in my direction, a smile curving his lips as his eyes crinkled at the corners. "Hello, ma'am. Dinner will be ready in about an hour." His long dark hair was pulled back into a ponytail. He wore a crisp white jacket with *Grand Wailea* embroidered on the left side in red.

"Great! We'll go get ready." I followed Paige down the hall and we both went into our bedrooms. Three-quarters of an hour later, we reappeared wearing our new dresses. Mine was a soft white gauze with cap sleeves. I had left my hair damp so that it would curl up as it dried. I had a flower of purple and white over my right ear.

Paige and I headed for the lanai, where we met Aimee. I looked out over the ocean as the sun was beginning its descent. Aimee followed the direction of my gaze. "How do you get used to this?"

"I don't," Aimee answered. "I don't think I ever could. I'm afraid that the minute I begin to take it for granted that I'll become shallow. Like Marisol."

No matter how much time I spent in counseling, I would never resolve the feeling that came over me at the mention of Marisol's name. It made my blood boil and my heart ice over. The hair on the back of my neck raised up like a cat's does when facing a dog. My expression hardened, while my mood stiffened. I shot Aimee with daggers from my eyes.

"Aria, please don't look at me like that." Aimee approached me and put her arm around my shoulders. She gave me a gentle squeeze. "I promise if I ever get like Marisol you have my permission to kick my ass."

"I want in on that action," Paige chirped behind us. The comment made Aimee burst out laughing. She turned to Paige with a pointed finger. "You aren't allowed to touch me. I know you. You would do it just for fun!" She turned to me with a softened expression. "Only Aria."

The dynamic between my two friends was odd at times. They liked each other, but I felt like they could be catty too. I got the impression that there was some unspoken competition for my friendship. Aimee broke the playful tension by changing the subject. "I love your dress! Did you get that today?" I looked down at my dress and nodded. Aimee looked over at Paige. "Where's your sundress? You're so much more formal."

Paige's dress was cute. It was a black sleeveless shift with red flowers, not a flowy, off-the-shoulder style like mine and Aimee's. I had known Paige for a long time. She had her reasons for always dressing in more classic styles, but she wasn't about to get into a discussion with Aimee about fashion. The comment put her on the defensive. "Sundresses aren't my thing. You wear what you like, okay? I'm doing just fine." Her tone had an edge to it, but Aimee shrugged it off. Sometimes their love/hate relationship drove me crazy.

Aimee went to the kitchen and brought back a pitcher of some alcoholic concoction. She poured and handed a glass to each of us and then set the pitcher down on the table. "Let's go outside."

The sky was at the edge of night. Luscious stripes of orange, pink, and yellow streaked just above an inky line. The landscape spoke to the hopeless romantic in me and a longing to share something so beautiful sprung up within. I would have enjoyed an evening like this with Declan; but since I couldn't, I felt the need to let Aimee know that I appreciated her hospitality. I turned to her. She and Paige were chatting about something; I interrupted them. "Aimee, thank you." My voice held more emotion than I wanted to expose and my eyes welled. Sometimes, I hated that I got so emotional. I wiped at a runaway tear.

Concern washed over Aimee. "Are you okay?"

I nodded, waving a hand in front of my face. "I'm fine. Don't pay attention to me."

Neither Paige nor Aimee spoke. It was probably better that they didn't. The last thing I wanted to do was to talk about my feelings. That would only make me more emotional. *Damn him*! I took three deep breaths. "I just wanted to make sure that I thanked you. Hawaii is beautiful and I'm having such a good time. I want you to know that I appreciate you inviting us." I walked over to her and bussed her on the cheek.

As I moved back, she smiled. "Aww. You're sweet. We still have a few days. Enjoy them."

Paige's eyes volleyed between Aimee and me. "Me too, Aim. It was sweet of you to invite us." Her sincerity wasn't as heartfelt as mine, for sure. She held out her glass. "Your chef makes the best Mai Tais."

Aimee chuckled and rolled her eyes. Paige took the last sip of her drink and Aimee refilled her. As they started talking about an upcoming luau, I distanced myself to enjoy the night air.

The past few months had been tough. The EMDR therapy had most definitely worked and every single detail of what I had witnessed at the accident scene was now clear. Knowledge was a pow-

95

erful thing. Although my newfound awareness had freed me from guilt's grip, everything that had occurred that day now tainted my thoughts. I plagued myself with questions. *How to tell him? When to tell him? Should I tell him?* Every scenario that I played out in my mind ended with the same issue.

Would it matter?

Chapter 26

DECLAN

arter had two beers in his hand when he came out on the lanai. My brother owed me some answers. "Where's Blake?"

He pulled a lounge chair over next to the one I was straddling and placed a bottle by my foot. "Taking a shower. Are you pissed that I invited him?"

"No." I reached for the beer and took a drink.

"I thought that you could use the company. Some guy time." His eyes traveled to my leg. I was rubbing it, somewhat out of habit. "Is it bothering you?"

I swung my legs around to one side and moved to the lower end of the chair. "A little. Today was the first time in a long time that I stood on it all day." I continued to move my hand up and down my calf.

Carter raised his eyebrows, swirling the brown bottle around to draw my attention to it. You're not drinking this with pain meds, are you?

I gave him a dismissive look. "No. Stop being a babysitter."

"Hey! I know you've been cleaning up your act. I don't want to see you go back to where you were a few months ago."

"The one you just gave me is my first. I think I can handle that much, mother." I couldn't help the sarcasm that dripped from the words.

Carter gave me a look that soaked with the same sentiment. "Just checking. I don't want you to screw up the plans."

I was in no mood to engage in our usual verbal sparring. Instead, I wanted to feel him out. "So what's going on in that head of yours? Why did you bring Blake out here?"

"I told you. Guy time."

"Bullshit."

"Oh for God's sake, Declan. Does everything have to be complicated with you?" I gave him a hardened stare, but he continued. "You've just come from a place in your head where you were giving one-word answers and slipping into the bottom of a bottle every night. I thought you could use a little relaxation."

I wasn't buying it. "And?"

He paused, then with a sigh, confirmed my suspicion that something was going on. "And I thought Blake might be able to help us."

"Damn it, Carter! We don't need any help." I rolled my head from side to side to crack the tension that stiffened my neck. "You don't want to tell him anything. What if he slips up? Tells her that I'm not really into her? I've been trying to avoid him, not get all buddy-buddy."

"Fine. We don't involve him. Quit your bitching." I was thankful to have a resolution before Blake joined us. Carter, however, was giving me a once-over look. "What's up with you?"

I needed to follow my doctor's advice and not shut down on my brother. If I couldn't rely on Carter to be trustworthy, who could I trust? "I've just been thinking," I started, "about…everything." My brother could tell that this was difficult for me. "I'm glad I was able to work this week, you know? It's the first time I've been in front of a camera in a long time."

"How'd you do with that?"

His tone was sincere and I needed it to be. Exposing my true feelings made me more vulnerable than I was comfortable with. "Okay, I think. Physically it was a little challenging. I probably need more of it to get my stamina back to where it used to be, but at least I feel like I could support myself—and have something to offer Aria." I shrugged my shoulders. "I'll be honest. I didn't think they'd want me back."

"The clients or Aria?"

"Both," I answered.

Carter took a big gulp of his beer. I could tell by his expression that it ripped him up to think of anyone rejecting me. He always had my back. Nightmares, crazy co-workers, trying to return to work; he was always there. Carter's expression turned playful. "So you've been thinking. That's good. What's the plan?"

"With work?"

"No, asshole. With Aria."

"I don't know." My grip tightened on the bottle.

"You're not going to have any peace until you get her back, are you?" He examined my response. "You miss her."

"Just a little."

Carter sat back and pulled down each leg of his jeans. A smug expression crossed his features. "Yeah. I thought so."

I laughed. "You're so full of shit. I already told you I want Aria back. Don't act like you're all psychological, Dr. Phil."

The comparison to the television psychologist caused us both to laugh. Then Carter's expression turned thoughtful. He crossed his ankles and put his arm behind his head. As he rested it, he looked up at the stars. "I understand more than you think I do."

I looked over at him. "How so?"

"Well, first, you're my brother and I know you. You're like me in some ways, just as much as you're not like me in others. If I could share this with Lacey?" He stopped. The pain and longing that washed over him were nearly palpable. He looked over at me, his eyes full of hurt. "Let's just say I know you want to be with Aria right now." He lifted his beer to his lips, took a drink, and simultaneously swallowed the liquid and the lump in his throat. "Anyway, that's how I think, so I figured you'd be feeling the same."

Remorse pulled on me with a heavy weight. I searched for the right thing to say, but nothing would express the depth of what I felt. How many words did I need to find to accurately relay how idiotic and selfish I'd been? Although I was putting myself out there to help him bring some justice for Lacey's death, most of the time I made it all about me. The expression on Carter's face was pained and I'd forgotten how much of it my brother had borne. He had lost so much: our parents, his wife, and me almost. It made me realize that I still had work to do to be more selfless. In that respect, we were two sides of a coin. Carter gave of himself to everyone, while I did not. "Carter, I…" I struggled. Now wasn't the time to go into a lengthy dissertation about the merits of counseling and self-examination. Now was the time for me to give my brother one moment of pity for the thousands he'd given me. I took a deep breath and reached out to put my hand on his shoulder. We didn't look at each other, just out at the night. "You're right. Lacey would have loved it here."

Chapter 27

*F*lying had never excited Marisol, but first class made it more bearable. If Marchelle weren't able to be at her beck and call, the flight attendants would serve her needs. It was a necessity to have assistants at her disposal. She craved respect; demanded it, in fact. Since she was on the receiving end of customer service everywhere she went, she would accept nothing less than the one hundred percent effort she was due.

Marchelle did not travel with Marisol, but was always at the same destination. Marisol had used her for several years as her safety-net. A way to get around the paparazzi. As a semi-mute puppet, Marchelle was rarely allowed to talk. One or two words at most. Her purpose was that of an illusion. All she had to do was look as though she were Marisol traveling incognito. Wide brimmed hats and giant sunglasses were a constant in her wardrobe. So far, no one had discovered the secret. Although they were deemed identical at birth, Marisol believed that she was the more beautiful sister.

The two had been close when they were little girls. Their father, Carlos, had doted on them while they were babies because twins were so rare in the family and it gave him reason to boast of his virility. That changed once they were no longer cute toddlers, but inquisitive children. Then they suffered at his hands. Marisol, who was named Marianna after her grandmother, had a stronger will than her sister. She refused to allow Carlos to break her spirit. He would give her the harshest spankings and she wouldn't utter a sound. Only Marchelle felt the pain. Marisol's hurt and unshed tears were communicated through the twins' unique connection. This phenomenon did not escape their father. He had noted the distress on Marchelle's face when he disciplined Marisol. Implementing a different approach, he would then beat Marchelle as punishment for Marisol's transgressions. It worked for years until Marisol taught herself to steel against the feelings. Carlos continued the abusive treatment against Marchelle, even going so far as to burn her hand for touching an item on his desk. By then, Marisol had become numb and seeing someone suffer, or making them suffer herself, had no impact. Marisol had honed the skill well, mastering her indifference through her teen years. One night she decided that she'd had enough of Carlos. She watched the hallway for him to come home. Her siblings were asleep and everything was quiet in the house. Carlos came home drunk—very drunk. Completely intoxicated, he passed out. Marisol snuck down the hall and bided her time until she was confident that he wouldn't wake. She inched her way up his body until she straddled his chest. The muscles in her thighs burned as she spread her legs far enough that they didn't touch his skin. Fury stirred from deep within her belly and fed her strength with an excess of adrenaline. She held the pillow down on his face as he moved his head back and forth, his arms jerking in a clumsy, haphazard motion. The alcohol impaired his attempt to fight back as she held the edges tight on each side of his head. When he stopped moving, she felt no remorse, only pride. She was happy to be the one that had murdered him. At the funeral, Marisol had held her mother's hand as she cried. Many men from the cartel paid their respects. Everyone believed that he had died of a heart attack. Though she would never be able to boast, she had taken out the head of the largest drug cartel in South America. She was invincible.

After that day, Marisol reinvented herself. She told Marchelle that she didn't like the name Marianna anymore. Marianna was a girl who had been imprisoned by her father. Now she was free. Marianna chose a new name. Marisol. By definition, it meant sun and sky. No one could imprison the elements. She would never be bound again.

Because she was beautiful, Marisol expected to surround herself with beauty. She seized the opportunity to become a model in New York City. A few years later, she quietly brought Marchelle to the States. Marisol said that she needed her. Marchelle joined her, but Marisol insisted that no one know they were sisters. She ensured Marchelle's compliance by telling her that if the federal officials learned of her existence, they would send her back to Colombia. The threat was sufficient mental weight for her meek and mild sister. Marchelle did everything she could to make Marisol happy.

Marchelle had arrived in Hawaii a day before Marisol. As Marchelle unpacked and prepared for her twin's arrival, Marisol schemed to get Declan into bed. After months of filling his head with stories, her efforts would pay off and she would wear down any remaining resistance. Marisol's sexual talents were legendary. After she had him in bed, she would fuck him until he submitted to anything she wanted. She was a drug and she would never allow him to be satisfied. A smile crept across her lips. It would be fun to keep him on a short leash and parade him like a favorite pet. Images of Declan wanting her came to mind. If everything worked the way she wanted it to, they would return to New York arm-in-arm. Wouldn't the paparazzi love that!

Aria Chapter 28

Our many shopping excursions proved successful; Paige and I had considerably increased our summer wardrobe. I had even purchased a few things for my mom. Our wallets were now as light as the airy fabrics filling the closet. We concluded the day by hanging out at the beach. I had thought that all beaches were the same, but not here. The clouds hung lower to the horizon line and the water's blue had a soothing effect. Aimee was finishing with her photo shoots today and the wrap party was tonight. Paige and I had the same intent: go back to our room, shower and change, and wait for Aimee. However, once I entered my bedroom, my ambition and purpose fell victim to exhaustion, which washed over me like a tsunami wave. I crashed on the bed and didn't stir until I heard the slam of the front door.

"Anybody here?" Aimee's voice penetrated the closed entrance to my room. I pushed myself off of the bed and opened the door to peek through the crack. She was the definition of perfection, wearing a designer swimsuit and cover-up, her hair and make-up flawless.

Paige entered our suite from the balcony. "Hi, honey. How was your day?" Paige greeted Aimee.

Aimee swept her hand in an exaggerated s-shape in front of Paige. "Nice!" she said. Is that new?"

A grin appeared on Paige's lips and I smiled as I spied on them.

Paige wasn't accustomed to wearing something so fun and flirty. Her everyday outfit was what I called business elegant. She turned around in a full circle for Aimee. It touched my heart to see her guard down and her smile wide. Her eyes sparkled and her dimples were fully on display. Paige and Aimee's friendship had grown this past week and I watched the new dynamic with interest.

After a few moments of exchanging compliments, Aimee looked around the room. "Where's Aria?"

Paige jutted her chin toward my room. "I think she's still getting ready."

Aimee started toward my door. I closed it quickly and quietly and ran into the bathroom. "Aria! Come out!" Aimee yelled.

I grabbed the fluffy white robe from behind the hook on the back of the bathroom door. Shimmying out of my swimsuit, I kicked it into the corner. "Be right out!"

I left the bedroom and padded toward them in bare feet as I pulled the robe close. They both gave me a puzzled look. "Aren't you going to get ready?" Aimee asked. "The party's in an hour." She looked over at the large clock on the wall while Paige frowned at me.

I looked down and nervously pulled at the sleeves. "I'm not sure. I'm drained. I don't know if I'm really up for a night of partying."

Aimee shook her head, refusing to accept my response. "Oh, yes you are!" Her firm statement took both Paige and me by surprise. "You didn't come to one of the most beautiful places in the world so that you could miss out on a traditional luau. You're going to have fun tonight—even if I have to make you!"

Giving me a determined look that said she meant business, Paige stood at Aimee's side in agreement. There would be no living with them if I didn't go to this event. I narrowed my eyes. "You know, both of you are pushy." My accusation elicited a grin from my friends. Resigned to my fate, I turned and went back to my bedroom to get ready. I re-emerged forty-five minutes later.

"It's sickening how gorgeous you are." Paige's comment caused me to beam. "You didn't spend half as much time as we did to get ready and you look better than us both."

"Come on!" Aimee grabbed my hand and pulled me toward the door. "We're going to be late and we have drinks, food, and dancing waiting for us!"

"Yeah, girl! We've waited all week for this night!" Paige followed and closed the door behind us.

———◦◦◦———

Aimee's familiarity with most of the people in attendance at the party immediately put both Paige and me at ease. She introduced us to everyone and after a few drinks, conversations were flowing quite comfortably. I distanced myself and began mingling as Blake approached Paige so that the two of them could become reacquainted.

Everyone appeared to be enjoying the luau and I was delighting in the looks that I was receiving from a few of the men. As the socializing continued through hors d'oeuvres and dinner, traditional Hawaiian music traveled through the air on ocean breezes. Guests found their way to assigned tables, aided by tiki torches lighting the walkways. The stage was framed and covered with colorful floral creations. Steel drum and ukulele music began to play to indicate that the entertainment was about to begin. Paige, Aimee, and I were joined by Blake and the owner of the swimwear company, who was the host of the festivities. We were front and center for the show.

The skits and musical numbers completely fascinated me. The island women were strikingly beautiful as they performed their various forms of dance. Graceful and elegant, their hands swept back and forth, mimicking the ocean waves with the sway of their hips. The dancers pulled a few of the guests onstage and I was one of those selected to join in a dance. The ladies showed me how to perform the arm and hand gestures. Thankfully, the alcohol had loosened me up a little and I became a quick study with the hip motions. Then the tempo quickened and the male performers joined in. I found myself dancing with a very handsome and muscular Hawaiian man to the delight of the crowd cheering and applauding for us. Motivated by the music, I exaggerated my movements and shifted closer to my partner. He wasn't complaining that the distance between us was so close that it looked sensual. I let loose, wiggling, turning, and laughing. When I looked out into the audience for Paige and Aimee, I pivoted so quickly that I lost my balance and nearly fell off the stage. A strong hand gripped my arm, catching me before I did so. I focused to stop the spinning caused by a moment of vertigo and closed my hand over the wrist of the man holding me upright. As I looked up to thank my partner for saving me from an embarrassing fall on my butt, I locked eyes with heat and fire.

The intensity in Declan's eyes rendered me motionless and speechless. I froze on the stage. I couldn't tear my eyes from his. I couldn't breathe. Time stood still. Everything around me faded away. All I could hear was the pounding of my heart. As his eyes blazed into mine, my body reacted. Memory took control of every cell in my being. My skin tingled and my blood rushed like burning lava as I responded to his gaze. Although I had tried to convince myself that the feelings I had for him were under my control, my body had other plans.

Deprived of oxygen from the moment that I saw him, my body demanded air. I sucked in one deep breath and then two. Tears threatened and blurred my vision. I quickly and frantically searched for an escape and ripped my arm from his grasp. I rushed across the lawn toward the hotel and the safety of the suite. I had to get there before my emotions erupted. As I approached the entrance, the automatic doors opened and I bumped into someone as I ran through them. I didn't have the presence of mind to apologize. I kept running.

Chapter 29

Aria

I paced back and forth; the cold tile beneath my feet contrasted with my flaming anger. I needed to form a quick strategy to deal with the awkward way I had behaved at seeing Declan. Something to combat the conclusions that were undoubtedly developing because of my response. From the moment my eyes had found his, all rationale evaporated. My violent reaction had commingled with excitement, fear, and passion. Lost in the jumble of feelings and responses that I was experiencing, I barely heard the door opening. It had to be Aimee. She felt guilty and followed me to the room. How could she not warn me? She knew that he was in Hawaii and hadn't said a word.

An indignant air ignited within me. Syllables of accusation coiled tightly and I made ready to unleash them on Aimee. I started from my room and up the hall to confront her, the statement falling from my lips before I reached the foyer. "You knew he would be here!" The words were bullets and my emotions were the loaded gun. I turned the corner and locked eyes with the guilty party as I prepared to pull the trigger on another verbal assault. Instead, my breath was squeezed from my lungs, the tight band around my chest depriving me of oxygen.

"Yes, Aria. She did."

The sound of his deep baritone washed over me and I drifted to a place and time when the mere sound of his voice took me captive. We stood, our eyes locked, as weathered brown met icy blue. His gaze penetrated my heart and sliced it wide open. He closed the distance between us before I could take a much-needed breath, his hand cupping the back of my head. His fingers threaded through my hair as he pulled my lips to his. All coherent thought dissipated into impotent particles as our bodies crashed together with equal passion. We were thirsty for one another, a parchment created by time and distance. I willed for strength, but my body and mind fell victim to my desire. With a weak attempt, I pushed at his chest, but he held me tight until passion consumed us. I lost the battle as he moved his body against mine. I didn't want to think, only feel. All that mattered at this moment was holding onto him.

As all conscious thought liquefied into a puddle of desire, I moaned. I had missed the feel of Declan's hands. They traveled down my neck toward the small of my back, inciting sparks through to my marrow. The sound made him fierce and he kissed me harder, claiming my mouth and whatever remained of my will. He held me in an iron grip and maneuvered us both against the wall. My back hit with a force that caused me to gasp. He filled my mouth with his teasing tongue; the sweet torture incited heat at my core and my sex clenched with a vise grip. Months spent alone enduring his absence had made my body ravaged from the deprivation. Tears came unbidden, trailing down my cheeks and inching into our connection with their salty taste. His kiss was full of longing. With it, he erased months of neglect and hurt. He pulled back and looked deep into my eyes. I noticed the lines that had formed at the corners of his since I had last seen him. Each spoke of pain.

"I was such a fool." His voice was rough and barely above a whisper. I swallowed the lump in my throat. He captured and braced me with strong arms. I never wanted him to let go. His fingers traced my breasts and rib cage as his hands traveled down my side. The feel of him growing more rigid and demanding against me made me ache. Sexual tension had rendered our breathing erratic as desire stole the air from our lungs. His absence in my life had been excruciating, molesting me daily with thoughts of what could have been and what should have been. Now that I was in his arms, I could think of nothing else but his touch. For one brief moment Declan paused.

"You're mine, Aria. Despite all that's happened, that hasn't changed."

The intensity of his gaze made me go weak. My chin dropped and I felt his lips against my forehead. I struggled for words, the sound of my voice so soft that it was nearly undetectable. "You hurt me."

"I know." His tone spoke that he was wounded and I knew in that instant that he had suffered as much as I had. I wove my fingers into his hair and raised my chin, pulling his lips to mine. His admission soothed my soul; suddenly, I felt reborn. Pulling me close, he took free reign as his hands once again coasted over my form. Mine did the same as my palms moved lower and drifted over his back and chest. I fumbled with the fabric of his shirt, my reward the clicking sounds of buttons as they hit the tile floor. He nudged between my knees, separating my legs, and pressed himself against my thighs. My heart leaped as I felt the hard evidence that he wanted me as much as I did him. With a flip of my hem, his hands came beneath my dress and cupped my backside as he forcefully pulled me tighter. A low rumble escaped him as his thumbs played along the rim of my panties. I gasped as one hand trailed lower and slipped beneath the thin material at my core. He played there as he drove me higher and I took a ragged breath. Impatient with the barrier of clothing between us, he removed my dress in one quick motion. I lifted as he tugged my underwear down and over my hips, then helped him to shed his clothing quickly. My head fell back as he pressed his heat against me, the temperature of the room now blistering hot.

His hands gripped around each cheek and he carried me into the next room. I felt the glass beneath me as he set me down on the table. His lips marked me as he kissed and sucked from my mouth downward, until he had covered each sensitive spot. Goose bumps covered my skin as he pushed me back against the cold surface. His lips pressed against my core. Tingles graduated instantly to sparks of heat as I craved what only he could give. Declan was a master in the way he brought me to the edge, but refused to give me satisfaction. Oh God, how I had missed this. He licked and tasted as if I was a delicacy. A slight stirring of air chilled my skin as he removed his lips. They were quickly replaced by his rock hard presence as he pressed into me. I moaned as each inch stretched and filled me. He sheathed himself to the hilt just as my capacity stretched to its limit. I soaked him with desire as he stilled, allowing me to adjust to the feel of him. My eyes opened to narrow slits as I looked up into the face of the man that I knew would satisfy my craving. All I saw in his expression was a raw need.

Chapter 30

Aria

"Beautiful."

The deep rich sound of his voice made me shiver as he looked down at me. It was thick with need and my body was eager to satisfy it. I, too, was starving for what only he could give to me. Every cell screamed his name in the silence, begging him to make love to me. My deprivation for him had gone on for much too long and though I had no idea what would happen after this, all I cared about was now. My senses engaged as I feasted on the sight of him, inhaled the musky smell of his sex, and shivered beneath his touch. The need to hear his voice and taste him were met by his mouth as he groaned against my lips, kissing me long and hard. He scorched my skin with unbridled heat as he played with the tip of my breast and then took it into his mouth. He growled into my flesh as his hips began to move. He sucked, pulling hard on one nipple with his lips as his thumb teased the tip of the other. I closed my eyes, surrendering to the delightful sensations. His hands, his mouth, and his tongue orchestrated my response. Helplessly, I fell victim to his thrusts as they catapulted me higher. His rhythm quickened and intensified as he drove into me. My legs circled him, locking him between my thighs. I was transported to another place. My heart was pounding, my lungs gasping for air as a million stars exploded.

"Declan!"

Consumed, I screamed his name as he pounded into me with a roar of his own. Both of us had reached our end. There was nothing between us and I felt him empty himself inside of me. Our coupling was intoxicating, an addiction that I would never stop craving, even though I had tried to convince myself otherwise. I allowed myself to enjoy the bliss of every touch and caress as he relaxed his movements. I didn't want this moment to end, didn't want to lose our connection. I held him to me as his motions slowed against my sensitive flesh. Words were insufficient and unnecessary as I savored the slowing friction. I was no longer the woman he had met on the beach. The road we had traveled had made me strong. His body bent in half. Still inside of me, he pressed his lips against my ear.

"You're mine, Aria."

The words were a ragged whisper. The cold ground of indifference that I had been holding onto by sheer will now shattered beneath my true feelings. Weathered and distressed, my heart spoke only the truth; all of me—mind, body, and soul—belonged to Declan.

As I lay in his arms, I enjoyed a simple task that I had performed long ago. Lightly tracing my finger along the intricate lines etched in ink across his chest, petals of remembrance unfolded within me. The intimate indulgence calmed me just as it used to and I savored the familiarity of his skin beneath the tips of my fingers. The uncertainty of our reality caused me to press into the crook of his arm. I didn't want to think about anything except this moment and the sated enjoyment we shared. His arm tightened around me as he dozed and my mind wandered, despite my intentions. I didn't care how we had arrived here, I just never wanted the reunion to end. The breezes of the island gently caressed the palm trees, making a whooshing sound as they danced beneath a sky filled with a million stars. Blessing or curse, Declan was right here beside me. I felt more contentment than I'd experienced in many months.

"I've missed you." The dark velvet tone bathed me in contentment.

"I would say the same." I turned my face into him, breathing in the scent I loved. His hand gently followed the back of my head as he ran his fingers through my hair. He looked down at me, lingering, as he gazed into my eyes.

"I've missed this most of all. The satisfaction I feel when you're happy." His gaze intensified.

I laughed. "More than the sex?"

"More than the sex." He pulled me into his kiss. "Though the sex runs neck and neck for first place."

I turned on my side and his arm came around my ribs as he held me close. We shared silence, speaking only through touch. The reconnection was relished, evidenced by our movements. Words were unnecessary and unuttered for a time. I ran my hands over his chest and across his hips, touching him in sensitive places as I urged him to love me again. When he moved to face me, pain etched his expression as I saw him flinch. The reminder of his injury from when he saved me was a blatant slap. My heart squeezed as the painful memory pierced my heart. Guilt whipped me with torment. Declan caressed my jaw and tipped my chin as he forced me to look into his eyes.

"It's nothing." His voice was soft and soothing, but I wasn't convinced. His eyes filled with tenderness as he tried to set my mind at ease. "I promise, Aria. I'm fine."

His life was forever altered because of his sacrifice for me. I wanted to give him the same pleasure that he had given to me. Moving slightly, I adapted to suit his comfort. I raised up, lifting my leg and running it across his pelvis. I dragged my calf and knee across his skin to stroke his pleasure. Once I had straddled him, I lowered myself until my breasts scraped his chest. I placed my lips against his ear, crooning softly. "Let me."

He hesitated briefly, then relaxed against the pillows. I indulged every deliciously wicked thought and took pleasure as I brought it to us both. I touched and teased, over and over, until we shook from an exhaustive release. We stayed wrapped in each other's arms while the night passed and the sun appeared above the horizon line. His chest rose and fell with deep comfortable breaths as he surrendered to sleep. Exhaustion took me as well; but instead of peace, I was plagued with the question of *what now*?

Chapter 31

DECLAN

hen I opened my eyes, Aria was no longer in my arms. I struggled to get out of bed. I slipped on my boxers and went in search of her. Following the noise, I found my girl sitting at the table. She had ordered fruit, cheese, and more substantial food from room service, but she hadn't touched a thing. Staring out at the ocean, Aria absentmindedly stirred her coffee. As I approached, she turned her attention to me. Sitting beside her, I poured some coffee into a cup of my own. Though I felt more content than I had been in months, I detected tiny worry lines around her eyes. Her expression was somber. I wished I could tell her that everything was going to be okay, but nagging thoughts of Marisol contaminated me. If Marisol was as unstable as Carter believed she was, I couldn't risk Aria's safety. My only consolation was in knowing that once she was proven guilty and was in the custody of the authorities, I could move forward with Aria. Until then, I couldn't risk putting her in harm's way.

"How did you sleep?" There was an underlying edge to her voice.

"Fine. You?" I filled my plate with food without averting my attention from her. Her brow furrowed. Her gaze volleyed between looking down at the table and staring at me.

"Not so good." Her response was tense, her lips forming a tight line.

I hadn't worked everything out in my mind yet, but her safety was my first concern. "Why?"

"Because I'm not sure where this goes."

Our encounter hadn't been part of my plan. Though I was determined to have Aria back in my life, I had to put her safety before my desire. "Does it have to have a direction? Can't we just let it be for a while?" She took my question as a challenge, the puzzled look on her face a dead giveaway.

"Let it be?" She took a deep breath and looked down at her plate. "I guess we can, but given our history, I'd hoped this—last night—wasn't casual for you."

I put my fork down on the table and reached for her hand. When I took it into mine, she looked up at me. "This wasn't casual for me, Aria," I assured her. "You've never been casual to me." She exhaled, her shoulders relaxing as she did so. I dreaded what was to come next, but knew that I had to maintain a safe distance until this thing with Marisol was resolved. "Unfortunately, that poses a problem for me." The temperature in the room dropped as she chilled me with a cold glare.

"And exactly what problem would that be?" Enunciating each word, her question held an icy tone.

I waved my hand between the two of us. "You. Me. This. I don't want you to read more into it than there might be. We have to think about what we're getting into. I don't want past mistakes coming back to haunt us."

"So what exactly was this?" She crossed her arms over her chest and leaned back into the chair. Her stare accused me and I couldn't summon the right words to defend myself. How could I tell her that I was protecting her by keeping my distance? "Damn it, Aria! I didn't expect this to happen! I was trying for it not to happen." Her brows pulled together as she sucked in a breath. She looked as if I had slapped her.

"Wow! That's surprising. You sure as hell weren't trying to restrain yourself last night!"

"I didn't even know you were here! Shit!" I slapped my hand on the table. "Don't you get it? I was trying to protect you! I've been seeing someone at home. A counselor. Trying to sort out everything that happened, how I acted. I don't want you to get hurt again. I'm trying to protect you!"

"You sound like you're trying to buy yourself time. Why would I need protection?"

She was demanding an explanation, and although I tried, I couldn't seem to find the right words. "From all the shit that comes along with me, dammit!" I balled my hands into tight fists, taking measures to diffuse what had the potential to become a volatile situation. I took three deep breaths, weighing my words in a calmer voice. "And from me, from how all of this started in the first place. My not thinking about actions and consequences." I was trying to explain without lying to her, but the words came out like gibberish. "There are things—people—you might not understand. They'll never be the same—I'll never be the same." She was thoroughly confused. There was too much to decipher. It would take days. My brother. Marisol. My physical appearance. I had to feel her out. There were things I might never be able to do again. Simple things, like going for a run on the beach with her. I looked down at my leg, directing her attention to its mangled appearance. "What about this? Doesn't this bother you?"

Her expression softened as she started to move toward me. Was it tenderness or pity? I had to know. I put up my hand. "Stop." She paused, confusion washing over her face. "Don't you see, Aria? You don't deserve this. You also don't deserve all the bullshit that comes with a man like me. Look at what happened before. The paparazzi. The invasion of our privacy. Marisol." Her eyes misted with tears, tearing at both my heart and my conscience. "You deserve better."

She squared her shoulders. Moving ever so slowly, she crossed the room until she stood in front of me. Still seated, I tipped my face to look up at her. Conflicting emotions warred within me. I wanted to take her into my arms, but I denied myself. There would be time for that once I accomplished this one thing for my brother. We were at a standoff, neither of us saying a word as our eyes locked. I lifted my arms to hold her just as she moved.

SMACK!

The blow jarred me as it came directly across my face.

"How dare you!" Her voice was low and firm. "No one tells me what I deserve but me. You think I'm so shallow that I care about what your leg looks like? News flash. When I look at that scar, I see a man willing to risk his life for mine."

I stood up, reaching for her in an attempt at damage control. She slapped my hands away.

"No! Don't touch me!" She stomped away from me and came back with my clothes. I flinched when she threw the bundle at my face. "You mentioned Marisol. Maybe you've spent so much time with that bitch that you're as superficial as she is." She backed away, disgust coloring her expression. Her voice broke with emotion.

"Get out."

Aria Chapter 32

As I walked along the edge of the beach, the tears washed away my anger. My convoluted thoughts calmed with the help of the ocean breezes. I had to clear my head. I didn't understand Declan's mindset. He seemed convinced that he had it all figured out. Meanwhile, I thought he made no sense at all. My emotions toyed with me. Suspended between joy and sorrow, the memory of what had transpired in the last twenty-four hours tore at my heart. The feelings that remained were confusing. Only one thing was clear; I was still in love with him. The sound of someone approaching interrupted my thoughts. As I turned around, I saw Paige. She wore a troubled look. "I thought I'd find you here. Same water, a different ocean." She forced a smile, but the concern in her voice was unmistakable. I tucked my chin into my chest as she put her arm around my shoulder. The tender display caused a lump in my throat that I forced down to keep my emotions in check. "Are you okay? What happened? Aimee and I stayed with Carter and Blake last night. We thought there would be cause to celebrate this morning."

"I'm not sure," I confessed. "I'm trying to figure it out myself. There's something different about him. Last night I was with the Declan I know. This morning I didn't recognize him. It's as if he's developed a new persona since the accident. Does that make sense to you? The same, but different?" If anyone could understand Declan's behavior, it would be Paige. She had survived a tragedy of her own, albeit when she was very young. A melancholy mask covered her beautiful features, but only for a moment. She nodded.

"I think I might understand more than anyone else. Circumstances like what Declan went through—is still going through—don't heal in a way that the body does. Although the wounds mend, the mental recovery takes some time."

I looked up, blinking away the threatening tears. "I'm sorry. I must seem insensitive."

"Not at all. Only human."

Paige sat with me as I wiped my eyes and tried to regain my composure. I wasn't sure what to do, whether to try to talk to him or leave him alone. If he still loved me, he would come to me and try to work things out. But maybe Paige was right; he had to reconcile whatever it was he was going through before he could concentrate on us. "I know he still loves me." The words came softly. Paige pushed my hair over my shoulder and leaned her cheek against it.

"Time will tell, Aria. Time will tell."

Chapter 33

archelle was hidden away in an inconspicuous corner. Marisol had been in a terrible mood since returning from the party. She spoke aloud, but to no one in particular, staring into space as she ranted and raved. The words she spat were nearly unintelligible. Marchelle recognized the calculating and murderous tone. Her twin was becoming more like their father every day.

"He thought he would play me, did he? Go behind my back? He thought I wouldn't be there, so he went to her. Bastard!"

Marchelle cowered as her sister raged. Having been embarrassed at the party, Marisol felt she was made a fool. Her tone was unlike any her sister had heard before and it frightened her. Whenever Pappi had used the same tone, people turned up dead.

"What was I thinking? All that time I spent with him in the hospital. I wasted those days, damn him! He used me. He was broken and he played me at the same time he planned to get her back! Does he think I'm stupid? If he does, the son of a bitch is mistaken! I will never forgive him for this!"

She turned toward the mirror, pausing to look at her reflection. For a moment, Marchelle thought the rant was over; but as she looked at her sister, she saw Marisol's chest heaving with accelerated breaths.

"Aaaiiiiiiaaaa!"

Marchelle threw her arms over her head to protect her ears from the scream. Never had she heard Marisol yell like this. It was as if the gates of hell had ripped open and a million demons joined to form the awful sound. The mirror crashed, shards of glass tingling as they hit the floor.

"He'll pay for this—and so will that little bitch!"

Chapter 34

DECLAN

I returned to my cottage after Aria threw me out. Mercifully, Blake and Carter were absent. Someone, probably Carter, had left a full pot of coffee. I poured some into a cup and went outside to sift through my thoughts. Without exposing my brother's plan, how could I get Aria to believe that I wanted her back—get her to be patient? Out of the corner of my eye, I saw Carter and Blake walking down the beach toward me. I laid my head back against the lounge chair and closed my eyes. I had made such a mess of things with Aria. All I had wanted to do was explain.

"I didn't think I'd see you here," Carter said as he approached.

"Me either," Blake added.

I shrugged my shoulders. "Yeah, well, who could have predicted that Aria would be here?" Silence hung heavy in the air and as the two of them exchanged looks, I made a quick deduction. "What the hell? You knew?" Carter didn't answer at all, while Blake avoided my gaze. "Shit!" I sat up, rubbing at the tension in my neck muscles. I shook my head in disbelief. I looked up at both of them as pieces began to fall into place. "Were Paige and Aimee in on it?"

Carter nodded as he took a seat. "From the look of things, I'm guessing that it didn't go well." His comment brought back the fresh image of Aria throwing me out of her suite and I let out a huff. "Do you think she knows?" Carter asked.

"Hell no! She was as surprised as I was. She's going to kill you when she finds out."

"I'll take my chances," Carter answered. "Can I ask what happened?"

I threw my hands up in disgust. "I don't know. One minute we were all over each other and the next Aria kicked me out."

Blake took exception to my answer and gave me a cocky grin. "Bullshit. You had to screw something up."

"That's great," I countered. "You two get into something that isn't your business, and when it doesn't work out, you blame it on the victim."

Carter laughed. "Victim? That's a bit dramatic."

"Screw you!" I gave my brother a hard look.

Blake put up his hands in mock surrender. "Easy boys."

Carter leaned back in his chair, eyeballing me the whole time. "Seriously. Aria's not one to overreact. What did you do?"

My tone became defensive. "I honestly don't know. One minute everything was great. We..." I chose the next word carefully. "...reconnected. We were together all night. Even had breakfast together. While we were talking, I told her that we should take it slow. Not dive right back in."

Carter gave me an incredulous look. "Are you serious right now? Do you hear yourself?"

"Back off, Carter. You know all the shit we have going on with the Marisol thing. I don't want to drag Aria into that mess."

"So you slept with her and then told her you wanted to take it slow?"

The meaning of his words dawned on me. My head fell back as clarity set in. "Shit!"

"Shit is right, Dec," Blake interjected. "I've gotta side with Carter here."

"Shut up." Blake's convenient solidarity with my brother scratched at my nerves. Then it occurred to me that our secret plan to expose Marisol's guilt wasn't so secret. I looked at Carter. "You told him?" Carter nodded.

"He did," Blake confessed. "I'll help however I can. That still doesn't excuse what happened with Aria."

I wanted to punch his smug look right off his face. "Yeah, I know, but how am I not supposed to worry about that shit? I don't want Aria to get caught up in this." I looked over at Carter. "If what you suspect is true—if Marisol had something to do with Lacey's death, then why would I want to put a target on Aria's back?"

His expression told me that my reasoning carried weight. He mulled it over for a minute and then gave me a serious look. "You have to tell her."

"Like hell I will!" My jaw locked so tight that I thought I might break teeth. "You can think what you want, but I'm not letting Marisol use Aria for target practice."

"You don't have a choice. You could lose her for good," Carter countered.

I shook my head. "Absolutely not. This thing between Aria and me is still there. I know it. Last night confirmed it. If a little more time apart kills it, then at least I know she's safe."

"That's a big risk you're taking, brother." Carter's tone told me that he was torn between what he wanted me to do and what he thought I should do. I knew him well enough that if I said the word, he would let me nix our plan.

"I know, but I have to. Besides, it will give her time to think about the future. She might not want to be saddled with a cripple anyway and this gives her an out."

"Knock it off, Declan. I'm sick of hearing about that shit." Blake's comment drew the attention of both of us. His features hardened. "It is what it is, so shut the hell up about it. I think you cheapen Aria when you talk like that. It happened. Get over it. You've got a choice—move forward or rot. Chances are she doesn't give a damn about your leg. If she loves you as much as I think she does, you two will make it."

Mixed feelings warred inside of me. I needed to think. After last night, I no longer questioned if I wanted Aria back. I wanted her more than I cared to admit to either one of them. But did she want me?

Aria Chapter 35

The flight back to Maryland was long and quiet. After discovering that Paige and Aimee were part of a plan to reunite Declan and me, the three of us had argued. Since their intentions had gone awry, both were shadows of their usual selves. When Paige and I had returned to the suite after our conversation on the beach, she and Aimee had confessed. Although I understood their intentions, I struggled with what had transpired. Aimee had spoken as soon as Paige and I walked through the door.

"I'm so sorry. You have to believe me." I gave Aimee a puzzled look as she wrung her hands. She had guilt written all over her.

"What are you talking about?" I looked between her and Paige. When my other friend mirrored Aimee's expression, everything became clear. *"Oh my God! Really? You two?"*

"Yes. And Carter and Blake. We were trying to help." Paige's voice was more plea than confession.

My eyes widened. *"And just what did you think was going to happen? That we'd fall into each other's arms and everything would go back to the way it used to be?"* Anger edged my tone.

Aimee shrugged, her expression making me realize that she truly thought it could be that easy. *"I did, or at least, I hoped."*

Paige appeared more repentant, her demeanor sorrowful and her shoulders slumped. *"I don't know what I was thinking."*

I grabbed the box of tissues from the table and ripped out two. As I approached Aimee, she took them from me. She dabbed at her wet cheeks and then turned her attention to me. "What do you want me to say? I'm sorry."

"For God's sake, Aim, I thought it was you that had followed me back to the suite. When I went into the hallway, it was Declan. I don't even know how he got in here!" Her face was full of guilt. I rolled my eyes. "Really? You gave him a key?"

She grimaced in response. "I thought we were doing the right thing, because I think—no, I know—that he's still in love with you." Her eyes glistened with tears. "I also think that if you're honest, you love him too."

I had gone to bed after that. I didn't want to confront the truth in its raw form. No matter how much I had tried to hide them, my feelings were pulled from the shadows and became bathed in transparency. I just didn't know what I was going to do about it.

The last twenty-four hours had been tense, but the relationship between Aimee, Paige, and me was slowly returning to normal. My anger had abated and I began to think about what to do about Declan. I wasn't planning to push myself back into his life, but the night spent with him made me believe that there was something between the two of us that we could build on. I wouldn't have to wait long to see how we interacted. In their eagerness to change the subject to something other than Declan, Paige and Aimee had turned to another topic. I would see Declan again soon, as Carter had planned a benefit to establish a scholarship fund in Lacey's name. Both men were well aware of how close I had felt to Lacey and the girls informed me that I would find my invitation waiting when I got home. It was only a few weeks away, which was more than enough time for Declan to sort out his feelings. While we were in the air, they brought up the event again.

"So, are you going to go?" Aimee's question was much too eager and animated, causing me to chuckle.

"Yes, if, I receive an invitation."

Both girls squealed quietly. "This is great! We're going to have so much fun!" I threw Aimee a warning glance. Instantly, she deciphered the meaning. "I'm not going to do anything. I promise!" To accompany her defensive comment, she used her finger to make the sign of the cross over the area of her heart.

"Want to go shopping together?" Paige asked us both. "We'll invite Katherine, too. We can make a day of it."

My mood lifted. "I think that sounds like a great idea." The simple pastime that the four of us shared warmed me. I missed Katherine. "How is she doing?"

"She's good," Aimee answered. "She's been incredibly busy with planning this. She'll love the excuse to break away for a little while."

"She's doing the planning? Wow." I felt a twinge of pity. A benefit like the girls were describing was quite the undertaking. "Does she need help? I mean, they can't be hoping for all of the money to come from ticket sales."

"Some from ticket sales, yes," Paige interjected, "but she's received donations for silent auction items. Aimee and I have been helping her with that. I've approached some of my business clients and Aimee certainly has connections. We have items for bid that start as simple as dinner for two at a restaurant to a week's vacation on a private island. What we were going for was to try and fit every budget so that we would have lots of bids." She smiled. "Carter has no idea. We're hoping to blow him away."

I became lost in memories. Lacey had been gracious and tender-hearted, as well as outspoken and practical. The whole concept of helping kids would have given her so much pleasure. "This is such a great idea. I'm so glad Carter thought of it."

Paige tipped her head toward Aimee. "It wasn't Carter. It was this one." Modesty caused a flush in Aimee's cheeks as she cast her eyes down.

"Really?" I asked.

"I just helped Carter." She gently shook her head back and forth to dispute Paige's comment.

"Yes," Paige interjected, "and you recruited me and some others. You pulled this together as much as Katherine did."

I reached across Paige's lap to Aimee's seat. Taking her hand, I gave it a gentle squeeze. "Thank you." Her eyes softened as her expression became tender. "I'm so glad that Lacey met you. You're a good friend to Carter."

Chapter

Declan

36

*C*arter, Blake, and I returned from Hawaii one day sooner than expected. On the flight home, Carter expressed more about his concerns to Blake. He was hoping that Blake wouldn't betray his confidence to Marisol, but would keep an eye on her. Blake was in an excellent position to provide assistance for Carter's purposes without raising too much suspicion.

The day after our return, we made a trip to the State Police Barracks. Captain Jax had agreed to meet with us and update Carter on the details of the investigation into Lacey's death. There was an air of trepidation as we approached. As Carter pulled open the door, I noticed how tense he was. Lacey's death wasn't a good topic for anyone and I couldn't help but feel a sense of heaviness for my brother. We followed Carter as he greeted the Captain with an extended arm. Once they shook hands, he looked back at us.

"Thanks for meeting with me." He tipped his head first in my direction, then toward Blake. "I think you've met my brother and this is Blake Matthews, a friend of the family." As Captain Jax took a seat behind his desk, we sat in front of him. "If you don't mind, I'd like them to hear whatever it is you have to tell me."

The Captain opened a weathered black leather case containing his reading glasses. He adjusted them and picked up a pile of papers, spinning them in our direction. He separated a few copies that appeared to be of photos. "This is what we have here." He pointed a knotted finger to one paper in particular. "It's a grainy picture. It was taken from security camera footage." He looked up, his eyebrows arching. "You've got this one already?" Carter nodded, so the officer continued. "Not the best equipment for sure. The images aren't clear and when we try to enlarge them, they get worse."

"I've studied this, Cap. This woman looks familiar. That being said, I know that we need evidence to bring her in for questioning." There was hesitancy in Carter's voice.

The older man sank back into his chair, peering over the top of his glasses. "We went through all the paperwork for that date. The car was registered to a Ms. Vencedor. Does that name ring a bell?"

The three of us exchanged puzzled glances. "Vencedor? You're sure?"

Captain Jax nodded.

"No sir," Carter answered. "Don't know anyone by that name."

The Captain sighed deeply. "There isn't much I can do, Carter. Apparently, when the car was returned, there was some damage on the front end. Her story was that she clipped a deer. One of our officers had stopped at the car rental place, probably to shoot the shit with the girl working the desk. She told him about it and he went to check it out to make sure that traffic wasn't impeded. There was a dead deer over to the side of the road. I spoke to the girl working that day also and she said the woman paid cash for the rental and the damage. Of course, none of us were paying much attention to a dead deer because Lacey had just died. You know how deer dart out of the woods. They just did the body work and that was the end of it."

Carter's anger flared, crimson heat creeping up his neck. "Whoever was working this case was slacking," he snapped. "Nobody put two and two together? They dropped the ball!"

Captain Jax was defensive. "If there had been anyone on that road who could have been a witness this would have panned out better. The only thing we have is a poor quality picture of a woman who might be the woman who rented that car. That's not a helluva lot to go on."

Carter wasn't about to go head-to-head with a superior, but I was concerned that frustration could cloud his judgment. His body stiffened. I reached over and put my hand on his forearm, gripping tightly. I saw the angry tic in his jaw when he looked at me, but the action was enough to get his attention. He took a deep breath before addressing the Captain.

"Thank you. It's obvious that this is an emotional issue." He stood and adjusted his posture before again shaking the older man's hand. That was our cue that it was time to leave.

"You're welcome. Sorry I couldn't be of more help. You have my word, if anything new comes up, I'll contact you."

Carter didn't say anything until we were outside of the building; then he turned to me. "I was handling it. What was that about?"

"Yeah, it looked like you were handling it. You were ready to let loose on him and that would have gotten you nowhere." Carter let out a huff to dispute me. "I did think of something while we were in there."

"What?" The word was thick with sarcasm, but I ignored it.

"I think that there might be a way to catch her—if it was her."

Carter narrowed his eyes, nearly glaring at me. "How?"

"Get in the car," I said as I opened the door. "I'll explain while we drive."

Chapter 37

*M*arisol had arrived at the house without inconvenience. The directions from Mr. Dietz were particularly accurate. Of all of the properties she owned under The Vencedor Corporation, she liked this one the best. It was the most secluded. The driveway was very long and the last quarter mile of the route didn't get any traffic. No one would come down this road who wasn't directly going to this address. It was perfect for the purpose she had in mind. She praised herself for being such an attentive businesswoman. It had been a smart decision to inspect each of her properties personally. She always chose to go alone, not wanting to chance running into Paige or Aria. Once she gave her approval, Mr. Dietz relayed instructions to them over the phone. All checks were cut through the corporation, assuring her anonymity.

As she walked through the house, she admired its perfection. An ocean view because Declan would like it, seclusion because she needed it. The structure wasn't enormous, but it was certainly adequate. Once she had Declan all to herself, she would make him believe that she chose it for him. She would create the illusion to make him think that she did all of this for him because she loved him. Aria would no longer be an issue for either of them. Marisol admired the handiwork that had gone into transforming the run-down house into a masterpiece. The irony that Aria was the architect of her own tomb gave her satisfaction. Images came to mind of how she would extract her retribution. She would dispose of the beach bitch. Of course Declan would be hurt; his ego delivered a massive blow. Marisol would then console him, giving him comfort and security. It didn't matter how long it would take, but he would fall in love with her; every man did. Then she would crush him. Goose bumps raised on her tan skin. The mind was very powerful. As the mental image of what would occur to ensure the destruction of Declan and Aria, she thrilled with a rush of pleasure.

Chapter 38

DECLAN

"What do you mean by you're in love with her, but you can't be with her?" Jeannie's tone was sharp. She slew me as she enunciated each word in a machete-like slice. "You made a promise to me that you wouldn't hurt her again."

For the first time in my life, I understood with complete clarity what people meant when they described mothers as lionesses protecting their cubs. Aria's mom wasn't large in stature, but her anger shadowed me. A sizeable lump formed in my throat, nearly choking me. My words were staggered as I issued a plea. "I'm in love with her. I'm fairly sure that she still loves me—but you have to trust me. You can't tell her."

"Stop being so cryptic and spit it out! If you're going to play games with my daughter, then I'll have nothing to do with you. I'll use any influence I have to persuade her to stay away from you. Anything to ensure that she doesn't get hurt—again."

"Jeannie, you have to trust me."

Disbelief registered in her expression. She shook her head at him, rising from her chair. "No, I don't. Not when it comes to my daughter."

I moved in front of her, blocking her way.

"Move Declan, or I'll move you myself!"

"Jeannie, please." My words were soft and calm. "If you'll give me a chance, I'd like to explain."

Her lips were a tight line, her expression hard. After a brief standoff, Jeannie went back to her chair and sat down. "Talk," she directed.

I sat down across from her and leaned forward, arms resting on the top of my thighs. I took a breath. "Do you remember Lacey? Carter's wife?"

"Yes. You're going off topic." Her tone was thick with impatience. "Besides, Lacey loved Aria. I don't think she would approve of the way you're treating her."

I nodded. "You're right; she did love Aria. Bear with me." I paused and looked down at the floor. I wrung my hands. No matter how I said this, it wouldn't be easy for Jeannie to hear. Taking another deep breath, my eyes found hers. "The reason I can't be with Aria is that Carter and I think that Marisol may have had something to do with Lacey's death."

Shock registered on Jeannie's face and for a moment she was dumbstruck. All color drained from her face as she fell back in the chair. Her gaze dropped to her lap as the air left her lungs. "Oh my God..." I let her digest that information for a moment. When she finally looked up, her expression was a mix of disbelief and fear. "Do you think she would hurt Aria?"

I inched forward and reached for her hand. "We don't know for sure, but I can't take that chance." Jeannie, still at a loss for words, struggled with her emotions. I made an attempt to reassure her, my words soft and comforting as I held her hand tight. "I love your daughter—am in love with her. When Aria comes back into my life, I want it to be forever. How can I risk putting her in Marisol's crosshairs if she's capable of murder?" Terror flashed through her eyes. Again I tried to calm her. "The police don't have any evidence yet."

"Then why..."

I interrupted her. "I don't know, but Carter believes it. The information we have is minimal. He has a photo that barely resembles a woman; but I have to admit, the silhouette looks like Marisol. On the day that Lacey died, this woman turned in a freshly washed car with some dents in the front end. She said that she hit a deer. There are no credit card records because she paid cash and gave them extra to have the damage fixed." I shrugged. "I know it doesn't make sense. In a big city, they have their computers networked and it might have sent up a red flag. Deep Creek doesn't have that technology. The connection between the two things wasn't made at the time."

"What happens now?"

"Now we gain Marisol's trust. That's where I come in. I'm the only one who can get close to her; hopefully so close that she'll slip up. I have to make her think that I'm interested in her to gain her confidence."

"Interested in her? As in a relationship?" Jeannie shook her head. "No."

"I have to. There's no other way. And the reason that you can't tell Aria is that Marisol will be watching her for a reaction. It has to be genuine."

"Then what? It will be all over the papers that you're with Marisol? Publicly humiliate my daughter?"

"That's not my intent, but if it puts Marisol in jail where she can't hurt Aria, then I'd rather have her safe—even if she never wants to see me again." Emotion bubbled inside of me at the prospect of not having Aria in my life.

Jeannie studied me, her eyes reading me as thoroughly as a polygraph. Then her expression softened. "I trust you; but know that if Aria comes to me hurt in any way by this, I'm not keeping this from her. I'll tell her everything that you've said to me."

Aria Chapter 39

octor Sumner looked at her watch for the second time. I was late for our appointment and she knew that it was out of character for me. "I apologize. I've been running behind all day." The doctor said nothing. I wasn't sure if it was some passive-aggressive bullshit to make me feel guilty. "I can leave if you want. Cancel for today. I don't want to throw your schedule off."

"No," Doctor Sumner replied. "We can start, but our time will be short." She gave me a pleasant smile. "So, how's everything?"

"Great—Good—I've been good." I hesitated for a moment, trying to find the right way to voice my discovery. "I do have a few things that I wanted to bring up—to get your thoughts." She waited patiently and quietly. "I ran into Declan on my trip. We slept together." Doctor Sumner's eyebrows arched. "Yeah, I knew that would surprise you." I tucked my feet beneath me. "It was a good thing…and a bad thing."

"How so?"

"Well, I know for sure that he still loves me—and I know that I'm still in love with him." The doctor's analytical expression begged a silent question. Knowing her as well as I did, I answered. "Yes. I'm sure."

"So the two of you are back together?"

"No, but I believe we will be. I'm hopeful, but realistic. There's no reason to worry about that, but something else has come up. Something more serious and I'm concerned."

"Oh, and what is that?"

"I remember what happened. Everything."

"I think that's a good thing. Once the truth is revealed, it can't hinder whatever will happen in the future with the two of you." Doctor Sumner described a situation that sounded so easy, but the knowledge I possessed burdened me with its murky oppression.

"Aria, the goal of counseling was to help you sort through all that happened. You wanted to remember the truth and you have. What about it disturbs you?"

My stomach twisted, anxiety swirling inside like a riptide. I knew what I had to do. However, the many scenarios I played out in my mind rose within me in angst-filled waves. I turned to my therapist, my shoulders slumping as I got caught up in the emotional undertow. "In this instance, I don't think the truth will set anybody free."

Chapter 40

DECLAN

I absentmindedly drove to the little shop that Aria and I used to frequent. Since Hawaii, I had made an effort to commit every moment I had spent with Aria to memory. Now, instead of only bitter fragmented recollections that had bankrupted me, I could replenish my emotional reserves with thoughts of her. I held onto the intent to rectify our relationship. Although I had almost undermined my happiness, I was hopeful that we were going to get a second chance. Life without her was frenzied and out of control. I wanted her back. I entered the shop feeling more optimistic than I had in quite some time. I wanted a small token to give to Aria to let her know that everything that happened in Hawaii meant something to me.

"Can I help you find something?" A cute clerk approached with a smile. She extended her hand. "Hi. I'm Cathy."

"Nice to meet you. Declan Sinclair." I swept a hand over the items in the glass case. "I need to get something for someone special. She's particularly fond of the beach. She says that the ocean soothes her. That it's her happy place."

"I have just the thing," Cathy said without hesitation. She took a few steps to one of the locked cases. The metal clicked when Cathy inserted her key. Closing it behind her, she approached me with a white box and flipped open the lid. Warmth filled my chest when she placed it on the counter. It was perfect for Aria.

"I'll take it."

Chapter 41

*M*arisol had invested heavily in her plan. Marchelle was a significant part of the strategy. "Where are you hiding? I know you're here." Marisol looked through each of the rooms as she walked toward the kitchen. Once there, she pulled out a corkscrew and a chilled bottle of wine. It only took a few moments for Marchelle to appear from whatever corner she had hidden in. She didn't look at her sister, only acknowledging her presence with a directive. "We need to talk."

Marchelle inched close behind her as Marisol poured a glass and took a seat in the living room. She took a sip and placed the glass on the table beside her. Then she looked at her sister. "You are aware that no one knows of your existence, aren't you?"

"Yes," Marchelle softly answered.

"They think you are me when they see you." Her tone softened. "You are a very special person. The reason I brought you here from Colombia is that you are unique. The similarities in our likenesses help me whenever I need to be in two places at once."

Marchelle, unsure of the stability of Marisol's tender mood, chewed nervously at her lip.

"Marchelle, because you are my sister, I couldn't leave you behind. I paid much money to bring you into the United States. In other words, I took great risks for you. You aren't legal, do you understand?"

With her eyes cast down to the floor, the meek twin nodded.

"I have something important coming up. It is the most important thing that I have ever asked of you. Although your English is limited, it is perfect for what I need you to do. The less you speak, the less anyone suspects that we are not the same."

Marchelle's head popped up. "Don't I do that already?"

"You do." Marisol gave her a pleasant smile.

The approval of her sister righted the axis in Marchelle's world. Pride swelled in her chest. "Whatever you need, tell me and I'll do it."

Looking down on her sister, Marisol gently patted her head. "Good girl."

Chapter 42

DECLAN

*T*he house was quiet. I didn't turn on any music. I wanted some time to myself to sit and stare out at the ocean. The memory of the first time that I saw Aria replayed in my mind. My heart remembered as well and clenched in my chest as I savored the moment. I mentally prepared for the upcoming benefit and the opportunity to see her again. All I could hope for was that our reconnection in Hawaii wasn't at risk of being completely severed.

"Where are you?" Carter shouted as he came in through the back door. I left my contemplations and entered through the front, meeting him in the kitchen. The back door opened again and Blake walked in, a garment bag slung over his shoulder.

"I brought your tux." He held the hanger out to Carter in his outstretched hand. "Declan's gift to you."

Carter unzipped the covering and eyed the formal black. He quirked his lip, his eyes never leaving the garment. "This is nice. Leave it to my baby brother to make sure I look good." He looked at me. "Thanks."

Blake crossed the kitchen, opened the refrigerator door, and grabbed some drinks. He took a few steps to hand one to Carter and me, but tripped over a potted plant. A puff of black dirt spilled over the top and fell to the floor. "Shit! Sorry, man. That pot's a monster!" He set the drinks down on the table's surface and righted the container.

"I trip over it all the time," Carter said. "I think he holds on to it because Aria liked it."

"It was a gift. Someone sent it for The Studio's opening." As I made to exit the kitchen, I nodded toward the refrigerator. "I'm going to get dressed. There's food in the fridge if you want something to hold you over until tonight." I went to my bedroom. As I closed the door, I heard my name and Aria's in the same sentence. I was curious about them talking behind my back, so I left it open a crack to eavesdrop.

"What do you think about them? Declan and Aria?" Blake asked.

"I don't know," Carter answered. "I haven't given them much thought. All the Marisol shit and the benefit have had my mind working overtime. I think they're good together, but who knows what'll happen."

"Yeah, I think so too. He was good with her." There was a pause in the conversation, then Blake spoke again. "What about you?"

"What about me?" Carter answered the question with a question. I detected the tense strain in his tone, but Blake didn't, or he would have shut up.

"Women, I mean," he inquired. "Have you dated anybody since your wife?"

"What?" He dressed the word in shock. I drew closer to the door. I had to admit; I was just as curious as Blake. "No—no. I'm not ready for that. Lacey's a hard act to follow."

"You can't compare all women to your wife, you know. No one's ever going to take her place." Blake stated the obvious.

"I know that."

Blake's tone softened. "You'll get back in the game when you're ready, man."

I heard my brother's heavy sigh. Knowing how much he loved

his wife, the sound lay like a burden on my heart.

"I'll never love another woman like I loved her." Sorrow weighed his words. The hardwood creaked as the sound of footsteps approached the other bedroom. "C'mon, man." As my brother addressed Blake, his voice bounced off the wall outside my door. "I don't want to be late for this shindig."

Aria Chapter 43

The Studio was stunning! Transformed for the benefit, brilliant puffballs of color added life to Declan's preferred industrial-style decor. Most of the interior furnishings had been removed and replaced for bar and catering purposes. The adjacent warehouse was rented for the night and a canvas covered walkway connected them. Twinkling white lights dressed the inside walls and ceilings, lending a magical glow to the white linen-covered tables and chairs. Just inside the door was a stunning enlarged photograph of Lacey. Each table held a miniature of the same photo in a square crystal vase. The vases were overstuffed with peonies in various shades of pink. The atmosphere was breathtaking, lending itself to romance. A lump formed in my throat as memories of Lacey swirled inside my mind. My heart was full as I got caught up in the setting. Tonight would be a beautiful tribute to a beautiful soul. A life cut tragically short.

"Hey girl! You look great!" From behind me, Katherine's familiar voice roused me from my melancholy. She pointed in the direction of the bandstand. "Our table is over there."

I hugged her. "This is beautiful. Lacey would have loved it."

A warm flush washed over her cheeks. "Thank you. I didn't know her, but I wish I had." She looked over my shoulder and around the room as people started to gather. "Where's your mom?"

"She's not feeling well, but she ordered me to give everyone a hug for her."

"Aww." Katherine's tone filled with regret. "Tell Jeannie that I hope she feels better and that I missed her tonight."

"I will," I promised. My eyes wandered around the room.

"You know, if you're worried about Declan, I put him at a different table than you."

I exhaled the breath I hadn't realized I was holding. "Tonight is about Lacey, not about me. Wherever you have me sitting is fine."

"That's good to hear," she laughed, "because he isn't far away." She watched me. It was only for a few seconds, but she inspected every detail of my body language. Purposefully, I remained detached, giving her no indication of my true feelings. "He's at the next table."

"Oh, good," I replied, my words delivered without skipping a beat. "That means I'm sitting close to Carter."

A wicked little smile formed at her lips. She was thirsty for my inner thoughts, especially since she was well aware of what had happened in Hawaii. I was all right with Declan sitting at the table next to me. I could handle close—just not too close. I wasn't sure how we would approach each other after the way we left things. Katherine's attention was soon diverted from me. I followed her gaze across the room as Aimee and Paige approached us. "I'm going to leave you with the girls. I need to finish a few more details on the silent auction items." She bussed my cheek. "See you soon, chica!" I watched as she skittered away, stopping to exchange hugs with Paige and Aimee before going in the opposite direction. I had the feeling that Declan and I had been prominent in their brief conversation. No matter. I had my big girl panties on.

"Hey!" Aimee was the first to greet me, swallowing me in a hug. Once she released me, she moved over to the side so that Paige could do the same.

"You look great!" Paige kissed my cheek. "If running makes you that hot, I'm envious!" She made an S figure as she pointed at me, the animated motion causing all three of us to laugh. We spent the next few minutes catching up with each other, especially about work and how impressed we were with Katherine's skills in pulling the event together. Aimee confirmed that Katherine promised to join us once she finished getting the silent auction set up.

"Speaking of the auctions," Paige said, "we have to check them out. I want to bid on a few. Several of my clients made donations."

"We should," Aimee agreed. "A few of Bella Matrix's accounts donated too."

In single file, we made our way through the transformed dining area. We passed under the canopy, as the crowd was moving in both directions. Katherine had placed the auction items in exhibition form, which caused people to go up and down the aisles like an amusement ride line at Disneyworld. The donations were already generous and overwhelming and my heart filled with joy for Carter. This event would certainly secure a good start for Lacey's Scholarship Fund. Just as I lifted a pen to bid on one of the items, a surge of electricity snapped my body to attention. My skin heated as the hair on the back of my neck teased me with excitement. Memory licked my desire as the scent of musk and cloves baited my emotions. I would know it anywhere. I sensed him and my traitorous body tingled with excitement. His rich baritone carried through the surrounding people as it caressed me with its sound.

"Hello, beautiful."

Chapter 44

DECLAN

"*Hello, Beautiful.*"

Those two words rekindled our connection, an invisible tether that clutched me from within and forced every synapse to respond. Phantom links in a chain of lust and longing bound us together. I watched as Aria stiffened her spine; she then braced herself with elegant poise as she turned and met my gaze.

"Hello."

The greeting cascaded from her water-colored lips. Though calm, the bottom one slightly trembled. I fought the urge to kiss her then and there. "Carter will be happy to see you." The omission of my own pleasure at the sight of her caused her to lift her chin proudly.

"Anything for Lacey." Her steeled posture contradicted her soft tone and the mix pulled at the longing I had submerged beneath my commitment to carry out my plan. I had promised myself that I wouldn't pursue Aria until the task was complete; but as she stood before me, I questioned my resolve. Flames of desire burned the edges of my intent, causing me to wonder if my well-thought out strategy would combust and incinerate beneath the heat of attraction.

"Is Jeannie here?" I shifted, hoping that the change in posture would gain me comfort elsewhere. The heat between us aroused me, making my slacks fit uncomfortably.

"No, I'm sorry to say that she isn't feeling well. I'll tell her you asked about her." Aria's eyes locked with mine. Emotion swirled like a hurricane in their blue depths. She lightly flicked her tongue across her bottom lip and my body responded. Though it was a clear indication of her nervousness, to me it was an aphrodisiac. It had been too long since I had held Aria in my sights. The slight detail, the minute tic, punished me with remembrance. Blood rushed and hardened me. *God! Was every little movement going to drive me crazy?* I diverted my attention so that I wouldn't give myself away, directing it toward the bidding table. I focused toward the item of her interest. "Are you bidding?" My question caused her to look down at the page which documented the bids.

"Maybe. A vacation to such a beautiful place seems like a good escape."

I didn't have a chance to learn the details of the package or to respond to her comment. Katherine approached from the central area, smiling as she looked between the two of us. Narrowing her eyes just slightly, she moved them back in my direction. "Carter's looking for you. Dinner is about to be served and he's a little nervous about his speech."

"I can only imagine how hard this is for him." Aria's comment was drenched with compassion. I wanted to hold her hand and give it a reassuring squeeze, but I dared not for fear I might be unable to stop at a simple touch.

"I'm going to check on him. See you both in a bit."

I found my brother locked in conversation with our special musical guest. As I approached, relief washed over him. "Dec, you know Melody."

"I do. It's good to see you again." I extended my hand, taking hers and giving her a peck on the cheek. "Thank you for agreeing to do this."

"My pleasure."

Aria and I loved the sweet sound of Melody Gardo's voice. Her story was moving. She, too, had been a victim of a hit and run, and after considerable time spent mending, she had found her voice in song. Carter and I took our seats as Melody excused herself to prepare for her performance. I placed my hand on Carter's shoulder. "Eat up, brother, and try to enjoy the night."

"Yeah, right." He inserted a finger between his neck and collar and ran it back and forth before picking up his fork.

I surveyed the room to gauge the attendees' satisfaction with dinner and was pleased with what I saw. Conversation flowed freely, a relaxed vibe transmitting through the air. Servers cleared the tables, drinks were refilled, and smiles were on most faces. My ears twitched at the sweet sounds of Aria's voice. Although I couldn't make out the words, her tone soothed me. I gazed over and smiled at her as the orchestra softly played a medley of relaxing tunes. I lost myself in the sight of her. Her hand was at her throat in a relaxed kind of way and desire again crept through my blood. I battled with my thoughts to keep them from bringing back images of our night in Hawaii. My eyes rested on her lips and a storm of lust made me thirst to kiss her. Confidence fell like raindrops as I knew that someday soon I would take my fill of her mouth. Everything was going according to plan. After checking out the room again, I returned my gaze to the next table to steal another glimpse of Aria. I was disappointed to see that she had tensed. Her chin was cocked and her fingers were tightly wrapped around her glass. An ominous look veiled her as black clouds shrouded her bright eyes. A deadly glare pulled her lips into a thin line. She steeled herself as she held back the storm, looking past me to the object of offense. I followed her line of sight, curious as to what had so quickly changed her mood. Turning slightly in my seat, I saw the reason for Aria's stress about four tables away from us. My whole body stiffened as the tasty food from dinner nearly soured in my stomach.

Marisol.

She was the lone woman seated amidst some of the wealthiest men in New York. The executives of one of the largest fragrance companies were dining with the woman whose narcissistic stench now polluted the sweet air of our event. *Shit!*

Chapter 45

DECLAN

*M*ercifully, the dark moment had been thrown a life preserver. Aria's tense expression lifted as everyone's attention was directed to the stage. Applause erupted as Melody was introduced. She was set to perform her song, *Our Love Is Easy*. The selection was at my request. Although the night was about Lacey, the tune was a favorite of mine and Aria's. The music swayed in a fluid, sultry beat as Melody's voice caressed the notes with her lyrics. A relaxed hush fell over the room as the audience slipped under her spell. Hopefully the relaxed mood would loosen the generosity of the crowd and there would be a hefty amount raised for the cause. As the phrase *our love is easy* rose and fell on the waves of Melody's beautiful vocal expertise, Aria looked over at me with a wistful glance. Recollection swam in her eyes in watery bits. The knowledge that only I could share those emotions with her filled me with longing. For a moment we were magnetized, but the evening was beginning to stagnate due to Marisol's evil poison.

When the song concluded, Melody thanked the crowd. I looked over at Carter. He had never been much of a public speaker, but chairing this event forced him to feel the fear and do it anyway. His speech could make or break the evening. I had no idea what he was about to say. I had asked him if he needed help, but he declined. As

Carter stepped up to the podium, the room erupted with applause and cheers. I had to admit that my brother looked great in a tux. Tonight was only the second time I'd seen him in one. The first was at his wedding. Carter raised his hand, his open palm directing everyone to settle down. He wrapped the fingers of his other hand around the neck of the sleek metal microphone, the sound crunching through the speakers. Once it was adjusted, I saw his chest rise and fall.

Inhale.

Exhale.

"Good evening." Carter's dark smoky tone quieted any remaining conversation at the tables. He paused until the room silenced completely and all attention was on him. "I'd like to thank all of you for attending tonight. For those of you that don't know me, I'm sure you know my brother, Declan. My name is Carter Sinclair and this evening's event is in memory of my late wife for a cause that was important to her. Education. Lacey Sinclair was a woman whose heart exceeded her small stature. Everyone who knew her loved her." His voice quivered through the words of the last sentence. He stopped for a moment, his composure threatened. My brother wasn't a man given to emotion and seeing his struggle was killing me. I shot up a silent prayer that he would make it through the speech without breaking down. He cleared his throat and bravely looked out at the crowd. His gaze shot to me. I nodded, silently telling him that I knew he could do this. He folded up the paper containing his notes and slipped it inside his jacket to the hidden pocket. His eyes scanned the perimeter of The Studio. When he opened his mouth to ad lib his words, his voice was firmer than before.

"Lacey loved kids—all kids, all ages. No matter where we went, one would find us—anywhere. Seriously." He quirked his lip and brow, indicating the hidden message that some of Lacey's students had interrupted a few moments that should have remained private. The chuckled response related that many people understood exactly what he meant. The reaction further relaxed him and he put his hand in his pants pocket. "I remember one time at the carnival in our town, Lacey and I were on the Ferris wheel. We were getting a little close—if you know what I mean. I had my arm around her, antici- pating that moment when we would reach the highest point. You all know the one, when it seems like you're the only two people on the top of the world. Just as we approached the peak, I saw that romantic look in Lacey's eyes and like any other red-blooded male, I leaned in to claim my kiss. Her lips were about an inch from mine when all of a sudden...'Hey, Mrs. Sinclair!'" He voiced the greeting in a high pitch. "Lacey looked back and three of her students were in the bucket behind us. Needless to say, it ruined the moment." Laughter erupted all around the room. He relished the joke and smiled at the memory. After everyone had enjoyed the funny picture he painted, they quieted down and he continued. "None of that mattered to Lacey. Wherever we were, whatever we were doing, she was always available to them. She loved them all. Lacey took her role seriously; she didn't just educate academically, she tried to teach the kids how to keep their bodies healthy. She taught them about nutrition and co- ordinated hiking and biking events." His voice trailed off. I knew the reason. A sad look filled his expression. "Lacey died while bike rid- ing. Some maniac ran her down and left her to die. She was taken from us too soon. Her killer is still on the loose. If I have anything to do with it, they'll be hunted down and held accountable for their ac- tions." His eyes went to Marisol and so did mine. Her reaction was slight. It was in her eyes. A dare for him to try. For the first time, I was one hundred percent convinced of her guilt. Anger bubbled in- side of me. I wanted to go over and knock that smug look right off her face. "Though my wife's life was short, it was impactful. All proceeds from this evening's event will go to The Lacey Sinclair Scholarship Fund. It is in memory of a woman who proved that a positive influence on a child can change the world."

A thunderous round of applause erupted, splintering the air. Carter invited me to come up alongside him as he continued speak- ing. "I couldn't have pulled any of this off without my brother." As I joined him, he gave me that smart-alecky look that older brothers always give their younger siblings. "Got anything to say?"

His invitation was unexpected, but I readily voiced my thought. I looked over at Aria. "All I can say is that I agree with you; good women are hard to find." The crowd clapped again and we spoke to them in unison. "We thank you all for coming." I looked at the scene in front of me. I saw two women who plagued me in differing ways. Marisol shot Aria a contemptuous look, but Aria's attention was on the stage. Marisol might be able to fool everyone else, but I could see the bitch in her rising. She was just biding her time, playing a part, until she got what she wanted. I just wasn't sure exactly what that was. My brother nudged me. His expression was flooded with appreciation. I wrapped my arms around him, slapping him on the back. "Good job, bro. Lacey would be proud."

"Thanks." His voice was more relaxed now that his task was complete. He broke our embrace. "I couldn't have done it without you."

I nodded, accepting his gratitude. As I followed him down the few steps from the stage, I looked around. Carter's suspicions had dug a deep grave and my mind wouldn't rest until I assured myself that Aria was safe. Table by table, I scanned the spectators as a spade full of darkness blackened my confidence. I couldn't find either Aria or Marisol.

Aria Chapter 46

I tucked my clutch bag beneath my arm and walked toward the exit. I had waited until Aimee's and Paige's attentions were diverted so that I would not be subject to their questions. Although I was proud of myself for weathering the evening thus far, I couldn't take much more. Carter's speech had left me at the mercy of my emotions. While Declan had pulled at my heartstrings, Marisol had cut them. I had nearly reached my car when I saw her approach from the shadows.

I took a quick glance around. We were alone. The parking lot was behind the building and music blared loudly from inside. No one would see or hear anything that happened between us. Hate launched arrows with dagger tips from Marisol as she approached me. I knew that I should be afraid. I wasn't. A panic attack should have been looming around the corners of my reason, ready to prickle my skin and steal my breath, but instead of predictable fear, I felt a rush of ferocity. It flew through my veins making me nearly drunk with a feeling of power. Months of angry bubbles fizzled and popped as they traveled through my arteries and veins coloring my blood with indignation. The frightened girl who had timidly walked into Doctor Sumner's office was reborn a warrior woman. As my memories of the events on the day of the accident were exposed within the therapist's walls, I had shed sweetness and light, my thoughts growing more nightshade. My rosy belief in the goodness of people was now jaded; however, it could not compare to the inky black of Marisol's soul. I steeled myself as her malicious gaze deflected off of the shield of self-righteousness with which I covered myself. "I saw you."

She froze as the meaning of my words dawned on her. I took a delicious bite of satisfaction when I saw the understanding in her eyes. "So the beach girl thinks she's a sandstorm." Marisol scrutinized up and down my form. There was only a small measure of distance between us and I could feel her slithering maleficence try to take control. Not today. Although I hadn't yet worked out the details, I would expose and ruin her.

"You think I'm not aware of your game?" As I took two steps closer to her, the parking lot lights illuminated my face. "You came into my home and tried to take what didn't belong to you."

"It doesn't matter," Marisol mocked. "I have him now. A man like him should be seen with someone like me, not you. Go back to your sandbox, Aria. I've won." Her entire body relaxed into a vapor of entitlement. In response, hate mixed with pity filled me.

"So that's what you think Declan is all about? What someone looks like? You're delusional. The man has more depth in his fingernail than you could ever understand. You make me sick."

Marisol laughed. A maniacal cackle ascended from her throat as she threw her head back. Her hair hung down her back, the dance of serpents moving down her spine in her curls. I questioned why anyone would think her beautiful, but the answer came quickly. The media had fed us all the same poison of the definition of the word beautiful. Her laughter ceased and she grew serious. "You'll never get him back. He doesn't love you."

"Maybe not, but I will always love him. Always look out for him. Rest assured that the only reason I haven't gone to the police is that I'll tell him first. Once he knows the truth about the accident, he'll want nothing to do with you. I'll never let you hurt him again." I heard footsteps approaching, and with each one, the pace quickened. Marisol turned.

"Oh, Declan! I'm so glad you're here." She feigned fear, the illusion just enough to put a question on his face. He looked at her and then at me.

"Aria?" His eyes never left mine, even when Marisol approached his side. She linked her arm through his. "What's going on?" he demanded, yet he didn't move away from Marisol. Even though I felt the pull between us, he stayed beside her. I didn't know what to make of it. Declan tried to take a step toward me, but Marisol held him in place. "Tell me what happened." His irritation was palpable. His chest expanded, rising and falling beneath a growing rage.

"She tried to attack me, that's what happened." My eyes darted toward Marisol as the lie fell from her lips. She cleverly twisted a heated conversation to seem like a verbal attack. As I looked back at Declan, his eyes narrowed.

"Is that true?"

Disgust filled me. He didn't know me at all if he believed that I would attack Marisol. I would never waste my time. I threw up my hands. "You two deserve each other. I'm done." I turned my back on them both as I walked toward my car. I didn't detect that someone was following me because I thought the sound of the crunching gravel was from my own feet. Suddenly fingers wrapped around my arm, jerking me around with the grip.

"You don't get off that easy." The familiar warm chocolate color of Declan's eyes was now nearly the color of midnight. Sparks ignited in his pupils. Everything about him spoke fury. His nostrils flared; his jaw was firmly set. Under different circumstances, I might have melted beneath the power; but instead, I wrenched my arm from his grasp. "Tell me what happened, dammit! I heard you when you said you loved me, so tell me!"

My thoughts went topsy-turvy. *He heard me?* Marisol ran toward us as we engaged in an eye war. She pulled at his arm, but he shook her off. Declan was nearly shaking, but from what, I didn't understand. His demand had scattered my thoughts and I couldn't read his reaction. I wasn't certain if I should be afraid for myself or for him.

"Just get out of here, Aria. Go!"

As Marisol ordered me away, the world around us moved in slow motion. I watched the scene in complete horror as Declan gripped his head in both hands and fell to the ground.

Chapter

Aria

47

I took a sip of my coffee as Paige's mouth fell open. Her shocked expression mimicked my own from the night before.

"Oh my God, Aria! What did you do?"

A twinge of guilt pinched me with pointy fingers. "What could I do?" I answered. "I caught his head before it hit the cement. He was out cold for a few minutes. I repeated his name over and over until he blinked. When he came to, he looked just as surprised as I was. I didn't even notice when Marisol left, but she wasn't there when I helped him stand up."

"Did he say what caused it? Has it happened before?" I detected worry in her tone.

Looking away from her and out of the coffee shop window, I replayed the memory, trying to note anything out of the ordinary. That is, anything other than the escalation of events between Marisol and me. "He assured me that it hasn't and refused to let me call an ambulance." I paused to take another sip, wrapping both hands around the cup for the secure warmth that inched through the ceramic glaze and into my fingers.

"How did you get him home?"

"Carter drove him." Although my mind swirled with reasons for Declan's reaction, I stated the facts to Paige rather than share my speculation. "I called him on my cell, then he and Blake came outside to help." I shrugged. "Declan had dusted himself off and was standing by the time they arrived. I know that he was mad at me because I told them not to let him drive, but he'll have to get over it." An indignant puff escaped. "It isn't the first time he's been mad at me."

"And Marisol just left?"

"She did. But then she miraculously re-appeared when Blake and Carter showed up. She started interrogating me in front of them as if she had never been there. I ignored her."

Paige's brows rose. "It was probably for the best not to engage her." She bent over to get something from her bag. "I almost forgot. A message came to my office from the attorney for The Vencedor Corporation. Somebody left their tools at one of the properties where your men were working. They want you to pick them up."

I took the message from her hand. "That's odd. My guys aren't that careless. They own their tools. They guard them with their life." I shrugged. "I'll swing by on my way home and get them."

Paige tore a piece of paper from a yellow notepad. "This is the combination for the lockbox. I have one on the doorknob of all of the properties until after the settlement. I have a key and so does someone from Vencedor. They must have been doing a walk-through to see if the work was complete."

I put the paper in the pocket of my jacket. "I'll stop by on my way home."

Rustling sounds rose from beneath the table and when Paige sat back up, she placed a sealed yellow envelope in front of me. Her expression was tender as her rose-colored fingertips slid it across the table. I looked from her face to it and then back out the window. Her voice was soft. "One more thing. I know you've been putting this off, but the papers are inside. I had them checked by my attorney, but you might want yours to look over them as well. Once you sign, The Studio will belong to Declan one hundred percent." As I continued to study the landscape, Paige watched me. "Talk to me, Aria. Are you having second thoughts?"

I turned to her, hesitation painting me with a wide brush. Stroke by stroke, I revisited my reasons and motives for severing business ties with Declan. "What if it was stress that made him go down like that? Something underlying that none of us are aware of? He wouldn't go to the hospital, but if there is something that he hasn't told us, something physical that stress triggers…" I shook my head as I looked down at my cup and picked at an imaginary chip. "I don't think I can do it."

"Yes, but what if it's all the pressure of unresolved issues? What if the matters that still sit unfinished and his hesitation and the possible complications of those things are what affects him? Wouldn't it be better for you to make it easier for him? The Studio belongs to him and it was never yours to keep. You should be proactive if you want him to have it."

I eyed her warily as she slid the envelope closer. I lifted it, pushed my finger beneath the clasp, and opened it, never taking my eyes off of her. I pulled out the papers and picked up the pen that she had also placed on the table. I flipped through the pages, not bothering to examine the contents. When I came to the last page, I penned my signature, stuck the contents back into the envelope, and handed it to her. "If I can't be with him, at least a part of me always will be. We built The Studio together."

Paige quietly took the envelope from my hand and placed it in her bag. She was well aware of the personal cost: the concession of not only a building, but a part of my life. Once she had readjusted her briefcase, she directed her attention back to me. "You know, he still cares for you." My conscience begged for relief from the weight of clarity. Sometimes the truth was a heavier burden than the freedom of ignorance. "This isn't all your fault, you know." Her tone was compassionate. "You can't keep blaming yourself."

"I know." The lock on the door where I hid away the actual events of the day of the accident made a clinking sound as the truth itched to be free. My trust in Paige made me slowly insert the key and turn it. "If I tell you something, would you keep it a secret? At least for now?"

She nodded, puzzlement filling every pore on her face.

I took a deep breath in and let it out. For the next few hours, I recanted in detail every moment of the day that changed Declan and me forever.

Aria Chapter 48

usic filtered the salty air as I drove with the top down on the Mustang. Once I had looked at the address on the paper Paige had given to me, I remembered the house. A beautiful structure with layered cedar shake siding, the white trim perfectly highlighted the dapple gray. The front of the cottage faced the ocean, the placement of the windows nearly making a smiley face as it looked to the sea. Beneath them were overstuffed window boxes in various hues of pink, giving the constructed face a rosy glow. Upon completion of the project, I had done a walk-through inspection. Memory usually served me well, but try as I might, I couldn't remember seeing any residual evidence that my men had been there. However, if the people from Vencedor said that tools were there, I would return them to their rightful owner.

As I drove down the coast, I re-examined the motive that had pushed me to sign off on The Studio. With the simple stroke of a pen, I had effectively amputated the remaining limb that entwined my life with Declan's. While I had told myself that I was doing this for him, the truth was that I wanted to make it easier on myself. I had used ink to deflect any confrontation with him, the black fluid bleeding my heart onto the page. With the few letters that spelled out my name, I had sent a message that I no longer wanted him in my life. Although my fingers had provided the notice with my signature, it warred with my heart. The Studio had been our baby and I had just signed away my parental rights.

Black met black as my tires swayed over the hips and curves of the long driveway. The front and back of the house welcomed guests into its entrances with patios of natural flagstone. As I exited the car, I noticed how the afternoon sun spotlighted the metallic specks. The music from the *Wizard of Oz* played through my head as I took each step. Dorothy had her yellow brick road; I had my sparkly silver walkway. At least Dorothy knew that she wanted to go home. I wasn't sure what I wanted.

I punched the numbers onto the keypad of the lockbox hanging from the oversized ebony door. With no furnishings or pictures to absorb sound, my footsteps echoed through the house. The *clip-clop* sound of my shoes boomeranged through the downstairs as I silently walked from room to room in search of tools. So far I had found nothing. Having gone through the front of the house, I made my way toward the back. A generous kitchen and family room existed in the rear with floor to ceiling windows so that the owners could enjoy the ever-changing oceanic vista. As I rounded the corner from the formal dining room to the kitchen, a lamp drew an arc of light on the beige wall. Someone was here. "Hello?"

I waited for a response, but none came. I quietly moved a little further inside. I peeked into the pantry and laundry room, but there was no evidence of an intruder. "Hello?" I repeated the greeting, this time louder than before. Again, no response. I tiptoed further inside and looked around the corner from the cooking area into the family area. A table and one chair were positioned in the middle of the room. *What the hell?*

A Hermes Birkin handbag in an angry shade of red sat on the floor, centered in front of the window. My stomach ran away and joined the circus, doing somersaults and flips which made me sick. My brain took on the role of ringmaster, blaring that I was walking into a tent full of madness. Something akin to terror clawed from within my head. The sinister sensation caused the hair on my scalp and neck to prickle. A lump formed in my throat and I didn't have enough spit to swallow it. Tentatively, I took a careful step back, then I took another. A sense of dread weighed down my feet. I knew I should run, but my legs wouldn't let me. Fear formed weights that hung from my knees and feet, nearly anchoring me to the floor. I tried to unmoor them, all the while keeping my eyes on the Birkin, as I expected it to jump up and attack me at any moment. I had nearly ceased breathing, only taking in shallow puffs of oxygen. Heat cascaded down my back as I inched away. I prayed that it was only a ray of sunshine, but prayers aren't always answered in the way you hope. Sometimes the devil snuffs them out before they reach heaven.

"Hello, Aria."

My vision splintered as the world went black.

Chapter 49

Heav'n has no rage,

like Love to Hatred turn'd.

Nor Hell a Fury,

like a woman scorn'd.

~ William Congreve, *The Mourning Bride*

Aria Chapter 50

I opened my eyes in a soulless black pit. Tarantulas danced around the rim, their legs raising and lowering in time with my breaths. I blinked several times, the searing ache in the back of my head slicing through my vision. *Is that someone's eyes?* Various shades of pain whitewashed my focus and I fluctuated between closing my lids tight and popping them open. I hoped that my tears would add enough fluid to the opaque scene to make it more transparent. I struggled to clear the confusion muddling my thoughts.

"Wakey, wakey."

A female voice taunted me, one that I vaguely recognized. The sound cut through the discombobulation, but the ominous tone with which the words were said filled me with fear.

"I'll get right to the heart of the matter; I've decided to kill you."

I recognized who was talking. The sound funneled down to my eardrum and immediately upended rational thought. Marisol's words made my heart take flight. It leaped from my chest to my throat and galloped at an unfamiliar rate as I filled with fear. The jump of accelerated beats made my lips tingle and my arms go weak as my blood pooled away and rushed to my feet. I wanted to run. I tried to stand, ready to obey the call. I wanted to get the hell away from here—away from her—but I couldn't. I was shackled hand and foot by what felt like cords, but was most likely rope. The pain in my head was once again activated by the sudden motion and threw my vision off kilter. I tried to focus and right my balance. Her words lacked emotion. They were monotone sounds that were more statements of fact than idea. The declaration that she was going to kill me punched me, the sting sending a rush of adrenaline that instigated a panic attack. Instinct screamed, the shrill sound forming from deep within my cerebral cortex. It pushed from inside of my skin, urging me to kick, rage, and yell with all my might. Unfortunately, I couldn't move. If I didn't calm down, I would give Marisol exactly what she wanted—my panic. I made a valiant attempt to bathe my brain in rational thought, shackling my fearful thoughts with bands of steeled resistance. Remembering my mantra, I sucked in three deep breaths, and then three more, and even three more after that. My only hope was that if I could keep Marisol talking long enough, maybe someone who knew me would notice my absence. It didn't matter who; I just needed to get the hell away from here. Away from Marisol. My quickly thrown together plan faced obstacles. No one would likely notice that I wasn't at work because it was the start of the weekend. I had no pending plans with friends or appointments with clients for two or three days. I could only hope that I mattered enough to be needed. *How do you entertain crazy?* I had to get creative. Find enough calm to keep her baited and talking. What Marisol liked talking about most was Marisol. Her attention span was short. She was self-absorbed. If I could focus my sentences and questions to keep her attention on herself and not on me, I might just stand a chance.

Marisol had walked to the table and then came back to stand in front of me. I looked up into her face. Tilting her head from side to side like a confused puppy dog, she backed up a step and squinted. "*No. Yo no lo veo.* I can't see it. I have no idea what Declan sees in you." She lifted her hand and took my chin into it. Squeezing painfully, she rotated my head. With a snapping motion, she flung my jaw out of her hand and to the left; then she backhanded me with an iron paw. Hurt electrified the inside of my mouth as my teeth abraded the tender skin. I refused to cry out. "Hurts, doesn't it? It's definitely going to leave a mark!" Her cavalier comment exposed her pleasure at my pain. "I'll make you a promise; it won't be the only mark you'll have today." Marisol's words plaited with my fear and anxiety to form a noose around my neck. I struggled to keep my breathing even. If I wanted to survive, I would need to reserve my strength. I had thought that I could endure anything after what happened with Declan, but this was different. I could only hope that I had the capacity to withstand Marisol's abuse.

"Mind if I smoke?" She pulled a cigarette out of a silver case and then clicked it shut, her metaphorical question subtly reminding me of who was in charge. She placed the rolled paper between her fingers and closed her lips around the filter. Removing a long matchstick from a paper box, she struck the tip on the side, right in front of my nose. The sulfur burned the inside of my nostrils, while a tiny spark flew through the air and hit my eyelid. My eyes slammed shut of their own accord. "Oh, I forgot," she taunted, waving the glowing red tip in front of my face. "I don't need your permission." Stars painfully exploded inside my head without warning. I felt my eyes roll to the back of my head as the blazing hot end of the lit cigarette ate through my skin, branding the base of my throat with Marisol's evil intentions.

Chapter 51

DECLAN

*V*oices in the lobby alerted me that I might not get out of the office soon. Today's schedule was overbooked. I made a mental note to talk to Katherine about it when she appeared at my door, escorting Paige.

"Hey. Can I come in?"

It seemed that everyone was making unannounced appearances today. Carter and Blake had arrived half an hour earlier. Despite irritation scratching, I couldn't be rude to any of them. Having just rebuilt relationships, I didn't want to jeopardize them by being a prick. I nodded, making a sweeping motion with my hand toward the two men. "If you don't mind joining this motley crew, be my guest."

Paige's bottom lip puckered in response to my half-hearted invitation. She walked up to my desk and opened her briefcase on the corner. She looked over her shoulder and smiled at my brother and Blake who were parked in the two chairs in front of my desk. I noticed Blake shifting in his seat. There was definite interest on his part, but then Paige was a beautiful woman. "Hi, guys. Sorry to interrupt." Slipping her hand inside the case, she filed through the contents and removed an envelope.

Blake didn't take his eyes off of her. He was blatantly eyeballing her like a hungry shark. "Not a problem, sweetheart. You can interrupt any time you want." Blake's tone offended me. I'd seen him act like this at clubs when he was trying to pick up women. I knew Aria wouldn't appreciate him talking to her friend that way and made a mental note to speak to him about it. I didn't need anything else complicating my efforts with Aria.

"I was trying to be polite. I thought you guys might be discussing something important."

"Nothing more important than you."

Blake was acting like a sleazebag. Paige's lips pulled tight as she grimaced. "Do you need to speak with me in private?" I brought her attention back to me, hoping she would ignore his asshole behavior. She turned her back to him.

"This is for you. From Aria." She stretched out her arm and waited for me to take the envelope from her grasp. Paige suddenly looked uncomfortable.

"From Aria?" I kept my eyes on her.

"Before you open it, remember what kind of person she is. She asked me to give this to you because she has a good heart. The girl doesn't have a spiteful bone in her body."

I noted the warning and ripped through the top seam with a letter opener. I pulled out the papers, quickly glancing at the first page. *Dammit!* My expression must have changed as my body tensed because silence fell over the room.

My brother interrupted. "What's wrong, Dec?"

I shook my head, disbelief creeping through the words on the page. "She's giving me The Studio."

"What are you talking about? I thought The Studio was yours?"

As I looked up, I saw a puzzled expression on both Carter's and Blake's faces. I swallowed the lump in my throat. My brother could always read me. His eyes widened and his mouth opened slightly. "Oh, hell." His eyes shifted to the side and he fell back in his chair.

"What's going on?" Blake's gaze bounced among the three of us.

"Aria and Declan are partners." Carter's statement was resigned.

"What are you talking about?" Blake asked.

"He's right. Aria and I are partners. We have been since the beginning."

Blake looked from me to my brother, waiting for more of an explanation. Carter offered one. "Aria found this building when Declan was on a shoot. She bought it for him." Blake's eyes shot wide open as he turned toward me. I smiled at the memory.

"It was the first time we fought." A sad smile formed as the scene played in my mind.

"Fought?" Paige's tone contradicted me, interrupting the recollection. "Blowout would be more like it." She waved her hand around the room. "That girl saw all of this in her mind's eye. Declan didn't trust her purchase or her vision. She was livid."

"I was pissed." I wrinkled my forehead. "Truth be told, I was also a little scared. Aria knew that, but she was fearless. She took a leap of faith and dragged me with her. I still can't believe how she transformed this place."

"She is amazing." Paige's posture straightened as pride shined in her statement. I nodded in agreement.

"You never told me that, Dec," Blake said.

I shrugged, returning my attention to the papers in my hand and speaking under my breath. "And now Aria wants to give it to me." I shook my head and looked up at Paige for clarification. "This isn't a sale contract; it's a title change. Why would she do that?"

Her eyes softened as her shoulders gave a little shrug. "She thinks it's the thing that matters the most to you and she wants you to have it free and clear."

I hesitated a moment and then stuffed the papers back into the envelope. "I'm not accepting it."

"She's not going to like that." Paige's disapproving tone made me chuckle.

"Then she'll have to get over it." I spun the envelope on the desktop back in Paige's direction. "Take it to her and tell her."

"Oh, no, I won't! You'll have to tell her yourself." Paige picked up her purse and removed her briefcase from my desk.

I pushed my chair back and stood up. As I grabbed my jacket, I spoke to Carter and Blake. "You guys get out of here. I'll see you tomorrow. I think I'm going to find Miss Aria and convince her that I'm not accepting her charity."

Entertaining their own ideas of what that confrontation would entail, everyone laughed. "You might want to call her first before you stop by," Paige related as we all gathered our things and moved toward the door. "She had to stop at one of the Vencedor houses before she went home."

The hair on my neck bristled as icy fingers ran a chill up my spine. Carter and Blake froze on the spot. A cold spell was cast over the room as the three of us looked at her in horror. Carter's investigation of Marisol had revealed that she had formed a corporation of the same name. We knew that this was not a coincidence. Paige was confused by our reaction. Dread filled me with the realization that Aria could be in danger. I wanted to be sure that I heard her right; the frigid words made my lips numb as they formed an ominous question. The tone of my voice revealed the depth of my fear.

"Did you say Vencedor?"

Aria

Chapter

52

I estimated that a few hours had passed and I was still Marisol's prisoner. My bladder screamed for relief, but I'd be damned if I'd wet myself and give her the satisfaction of my body's surrender to fear. My skin screamed in the spots where she had burned me with her cigarette. I bit the inside of my cheek to misdirect the pain she had caused and to take control of my own affliction. Marisol leaned back in her chair directly in front of me. Her posture reminded me of a scene from a movie with Sharon Stone. Flicking ashes at me, she took a deep drag. The smoke seeped from her teeth as she exhaled and smiled. Obviously, this was an amusing game for her.

"It's been a while since you got here." She leaned forward and studied my face. "You look a little pale. I can't have you passing out on me again." She placed her hand just above my knee and inched it up toward my thigh. I hated the involuntary goose bumps that formed beneath her fingertips, the remnants created in the wake of her evil touch. Her fingers traveled to where my leg bent toward my hip. I sucked in a breath as she pulled her hand back and dredged her fingernails beneath the edges of my seared flesh. The sharp pointy tips amplified the sensation of pain in the fresh burns. She placed the ball of her foot against the chair leg just above where my foot was tied. The side of her shoe slid against my ankle, my skin cringing as

I angled my leg in the opposite direction. Her eyes never left my face. She studied my reactions, all of which I tried to hide. This was one time when I desperately wished I could better conceal my emotions, but was sorely reminded that I couldn't even bluff in a simple card game. She detected my disgust and placed her foot full against my calf. She narrowed her eyes, the color a hollow black, and pushed against the chair as her hip rose from the seat. My neck snapped as I went flying backward. A painful thud reverberated as pain shot through my head. My top and bottom teeth clattered painfully against each other and my ears vibrated as the sensations of touch and sound collided. I felt a sharp prick against the back of my scalp and deduced that the skin had opened upon impact with the floor. The wooden chair that I was strapped to was tall, its ladder back more torture device than support since I'd been seated so long. My injuries battled for supremacy, each one throbbing for my attention. I had to stay calm and alert. I couldn't give in to the frightening demons trying to rip apart my psyche. I was afraid that the moment she thought she'd bested me that she would tire of the game and finish me off. My fear would not be offered up as a sacrifice to her insanity. Instead, I compartmentalized my painful thoughts, letting them scream inside my head and into my soul.

"Not like falling in the sand, is it, beach bitch?" Marisol stood over me, the scene above my eyes sliced in half by the hem of her skirt. Depending on where I placed my view, I either looked into her face or beneath the material to the top of her legs. She wasn't wearing underwear. She noticed my struggle. "Take a good look." She moved half a step forward, forcing me to look up her skirt. The shadow distorted my view of her smoothly waxed skin, which I had no desire to see. I closed my eyes. Marisol uttered an evil little laugh. "I'm giving you a complimentary view of what the world pays millions to see. This is what Declan likes to fuck." She bent at the knees, straddling my neck with her naked skin. Spreading her knees further apart, she pressed her weight against my throat. She leaned back, her folds separating against my windpipe. I struggled for breath as she pulled the fabric back to look at my face. "Awww, poor little beach girl." I struggled to maintain focus as I gasped for air. "You should know that I've undone some mighty men with this pussy. Men worth more money and power than you can imagine. I assure you; you're no match for them."

For the second time, I felt myself losing consciousness. If Marisol succeeded in suffocating me, I had to get the last word. "You won't get away with this." My voice was a hoarse whisper as the words strained beneath the struggle. Marisol grabbed the sides of my head with both hands. Her nails drove into my scalp as she grabbed my hair and pulled me upward. The pressure doubled at my throat as all efforts for oxygen halted. Her lips formed a sneer, her spittle popping into my face like overheated grease. The edges of my sight darkened as I retracted into blackness. "That's where you're wrong, Aria." She twisted her hands into my hair with just enough painful force to keep me conscious for another moment. Her slimy ebony words slid like deadly snakes through her gritted white teeth. "Who's going to stop me?"

Chapter 58

DECLAN

*P*aige could tell I was worried. "What's wrong?"

I felt the blood drain away from my face. I had been trying to coax Marisol into confessing her involvement in Lacey's death without success. She played innocent whenever I broached the subject of my brother or Lacey. Obviously, I had underestimated her acting ability. She had never let on that she had been at Deep Creek Lake or knew any details of Lacey's death. She hid her feelings in dark corners, webbing her emotions like a graceful spider. The idea that Aria had unknowingly walked into her trap made me sick. "Tell me that where she went was somewhere public like a restaurant or coffee shop."

"No, she went to a house. One of her guys left something there and someone from Vencedor found it during the walk through." She gave all of us a hard look. "Will someone please tell me what the hell is going on?"

I ignored her, instead looking over at Carter. He raised his hand to halt my racing thoughts. "Calm down, Dec. It could be nothing."

"But it could be something." My statement came out more harshly than I had intended. Aria went to Vencedor. Vencedor was Marisol. A deep dread weighed down my insides. "I can't take the chance."

Carter looked from me to Paige. "Do you have the address?"

"I don't, but the girls at the desk always write the messages in a book. There are two copies: one for the person and one for the company. I'm sure that I could find it at the office." Panic filled her eyes. "Is Aria in trouble?"

"I think so. Marisol owns the Vencedor Corporation."

A look came over Paige's face like someone had punched her in the stomach. A rush of air left her as she bent at the waist. "Oh my God." Her words were tainted with fear. "I've been working with The Vencedor Corporation for nearly a year. I didn't know."

Carter sprang to grab his keys. "We have to get to Paige's office to get that address." He grabbed Paige's wrist. "C'mon. We don't have time for this. You can feel bad later."

She stumbled as Carter pulled her toward the door; then her head snapped up and she cemented her feet. "Wait a minute!" She snatched her hand back from him and moved quickly to my desk. She lifted the briefcase up and began to rummage through it while she talked to us over her shoulder. "I think I might have something in here. Two houses involved with last minute details. I think I have another copy of the message. The receptionist knew I would have two different people following up on it. She duplicated it so I didn't have to rewrite it." Frantically, she removed and reviewed pieces of paper until, finally, she triumphantly held one up. "Found it!"

I rushed over to her and captured it from her hand. "Which address did Aria go to?"

"I don't know." Helplessness rendered her breathless.

I grabbed a pen, wrote down one of the addresses on a piece of paper, and then gave it to Carter. "You and Blake take this one; I'll take the other."

"Got it. Whoever gets to her first, call the other," Carter instructed.

"I'm coming with you." Paige quickened her steps and followed behind me.

I turned toward her, halting her. "No. You stay here with Katherine." Anger flashed in her eyes, but I preferred to have her safe than at risk. "We could be walking into a trap. I can't be worried about getting both you and Aria to safety." There was an argument in her expression, but I refused to engage. Time was of the essence if Marisol had Aria. My hope was that we were all overreacting, and if so, we could laugh about it later. Aria could be safe at home watching a movie, but I doubted it. My gut told me otherwise.

Chapter 54

Marchelle couldn't stop her silent tears. From her hiding place in the corner, she watched helplessly as Marisol extracted hateful revenge on the woman tied to the chair. Somehow this woman had angered her sister and was paying whatever price Marisol had set. Unfortunately for her twin's victim, the cost wasn't in dollars but in pain. Although Marchelle didn't speak it fluently, she comprehended most of the English language. Her mind raced. The last time Marisol had lost control, they were in a car in the country. She was angry that Declan Sinclair was going away with a woman other than her. Marisol had planned to intercept him and was driving Marchelle into town so that people would see her. Marisol had said that if things got ugly between her and Declan, Marchelle would be her alibi that she was in the same town, but somewhere else. It would be her word against his. Marisol never did confront him that day. Their plans had changed when she careened around a curve and hit the woman on the bike.

"Shit!" Marisol cussed and stopped the car. They had hit something, but Marchelle couldn't see what it was. "Stay here! I'll be right back." Having received her orders, Marchelle didn't move from her seat. The window was open and everything was quiet, except for bird songs and a calm wind whistling softly through the tree tops. She zeroed in on the clicking sound of Marisol's high heels.

She was a few feet from the car.

"Help me."

A feminine voice, filled with pain, carried through the air. Marchelle grabbed the door handle; her sense of compassion was tempting her to ignore her sister's words and rush to offer assistance.

"Please…"

The plea tore at Marchelle's heart. She prayed that Marisol would come back to the car to get her cell phone. It was an accident. She hadn't meant to hit the woman. After a moment, she heard the sound of Marisol's shoes as they approached the car. Marchelle stared at her sister as she slid behind the wheel and put the vehicle in drive. Her mouth dried up. The lump in her throat grew in size, as did the distance between them and the woman they had hurt. Marchelle opened her mouth to ask a question and Marisol's head spun in her direction before she had uttered a word. Her twin wore an angry glare so intense that it nearly stopped her heart.

"Don't you say a fucking word. I know what I'm doing."

They had never talked about it. Not one word of discussion between them had occurred, nor had an ounce of compassion been issued. That was the day that Marchelle's eyes had been opened to the evil heart of her twin. They may have been identical on the outside, but on the inside they were nothing alike. God had created them in front of a mirror, giving them the same nose, mouth, and eyes. Even their hair was identical, the same diameter of curl and the same texture. Their stature was so similar that they fit into the same clothes and shoes. There was only one thing that distinguished them on the day of their conception, setting them apart and exposing their real identities, not that anyone knew of Marchelle's existence. A game had been played by two powerful forces in the universe—perhaps a flip of a coin the moment before two infant girls came from heaven to earth, screaming from their mother's womb. The second that two daughters no longer relied on their mother's body to keep them both alive. That precious moment when their little eyes opened and they existed because of the most important organ inside their bodies: the heart.

The power of God pulsed through one. And through the other, the devil.

Aria Chapter 55

I wasn't sure how long I had been out, but I could tell that Marisol hadn't stopped hurting me while I was unconscious. When I opened my eyes, one obeyed and one did not. I could see only a sliver of light through the slit. The pain made my temple throb. Over and over, it pulsated as blood coursed through my head. I focused with my limited vision and saw that I had been returned to an upright position, but I wasn't in the same place where I had started. I looked down at the floor, noting the scrape marks in the new hardwood. The fresh scratches indicated that the chair had been dragged across the floor while I was in it. I turned my head. Though my vision was hazy, I saw that I was precariously perched inches away from a set of stairs. The steps led to the outside entrance at the back of the house, just off of the central patio. When I looked to the other side, I saw the edge of a large window in my peripheral vision and faintly heard the lap of the water connecting the property to the sea. No rays of sun filled the room. It was growing dark and I tensed further as I realized that with the night would come more terrors.

"Well, hello, sunshine. I'm so glad that you decided to rejoin our fun and games. As I'm sure you might have guessed, I played without you."

Her statement was confirmation that she had continued her assault while I was out cold. I opened my mouth to comment, but a jolt of pain shot through my face. It splintered in three directions as it headed to my eye, ear, and jaw. A tear escaped as I realized that my cheekbone was shattered. I gently closed my eyes, forcing myself to focus on staying alive. As I opened them again, I looked at Marisol. It was like looking into the eyes of hell. She was the embodiment of the beautiful side of evil. Her face was flawless like she had just had her make-up freshly done. Behind her on the table was a large mirror. I could see black handles all pointed in my direction. *Now she wants to do make-up?*

Marisol sensed my puzzled thoughts. "We're going to have a little make-up lesson." Her voice was animated, alerting me that she had descended to a new level of madness. I struggled to follow her movements, my sight unbalanced from my injuries. She turned her back to me, but I could see her hand. She had gathered an implement from the table and palmed it. She draped a white towel over that same hand and pulled her chair in front of mine. She studied me. I dropped my chin, but she grabbed the top of my head and pulled it up.

"Look at me." It was meant as an implicit threat-filled order, but I rebuked it by pulling in the opposite direction in an attempt to keep my chin down. She dropped my head and slapped my injured cheek. "I said look at me, you little bitch!"

Despite my attempt to quiet my cries, I groaned in pain. She placed her hand under my chin and lifted it. With just enough light in the room, the movement of her hand exposed a glint of metal. She had a knife. Fear raised its head like a sleeping dragon and I panicked, attempting to pull my face away from her, but she held fast. A cold sensation ran along my jawline, followed by an unfamiliar and strange prickling that I could only compare to pins and needles.

"I need to teach you about contouring." She pressed the blade in deeper and I screamed. Her hand stilled. She pulled her arm back. I was afraid to close my eyes, but equally afraid to keep them open. "That's funny. Both you and Carter's wife have the same expression." She shrugged with the observation. "Maybe it doesn't have anything to do with you. Maybe everyone sports the same expression when they're close to death."

Reality doused me in an acid bath, nearly drowning me with the implication. "What?" I croaked the question, a sob stealing my voice.

"You and Lacey Sinclair," she clarified. "I stood above her just like I am doing with you. I didn't realize it at the time, but she was dying." She gave a little shrug as her lips curved into a smile. "You know what that means, don't you, Aria?" She placed the knife against my throat. My pulse quickened to the beat of a thousand drums. She drew near. She breathed me in, sliding her nose up the length of my neck. Like an animal sampling the taste of its prey before a kill, she ran her tongue along the rim of my ear. My chest was caving in on itself. I could barely take a breath as fear crushed me. She whispered to me, her words hopscotching over my skin as they roared my fate on a puff of air.

"Die, bitch."

Chapter 56

DECLAN

I didn't know why the door had been left unlocked, but when I approached, it was ajar. I heard voices and took quiet steps in that direction. Marisol didn't see me as I approached. In the nanosecond between my appearance and seeing the knife at Aria's throat, I lived a lifetime. And when your life flashes before your eyes, you are filled with many things. Hopes, regrets; both of those came together and caused a cosmic explosion inside. My reaction wasn't something I could control. Basic survival instinct filled and possessed me. Not for me, for Aria.

"Put. It. Down."

The words came out as a command. A directive. I took a quick glance at Aria. She didn't turn her head toward me, but I could read her body language. Relief sagged her shoulders. I promised myself that I would walk out of here with Aria, even if Marisol's dead body paved our path.

Marisol's hand fell to her side as she stood and turned toward me. She released her hold on Aria's head and it fell limp to her chest. She narrowed her eyes, her countenance a study of evil. "So glad you could join us." Her malicious tone grated my ears.

"Let her go. She's not who you want." I took a few steps closer.

"On the contrary, she is exactly who I want." Marisol pointed at me, the knife still in her hand. She dragged her steps a bit as she

191

came toward me. I could only guess from Aria's appearance that Marisol had been at this for some time. "*She* is the reason for the sudden drop in our popularity. *She* is the reason that we no longer go to parties. *She* is the reason you've lost interest in me. So yes, *she* is who I want. Once she is gone, your focus will be where it should have always been—on me."

She was mad. Crazy. Certifiable. Although I stayed calm on the outside, my heart became a race car, zooming my blood through my veins. I strode a few more steps toward her as I controlled my rage. She was still much too close to Aria for my comfort. "My focus has always been on you. I know that without you, no one would want me." Marisol cocked her head to the side, not trusting my words, but intrigued by the content. "I know that it started out as an illusion, but I do enjoy our time together. And when Aria deserted me in the hospital, you were there for me. You reminded me of what my life was like before I became distracted. I don't know what came over me when I went to the beach. I wasn't thinking straight because I was exhausted. Aria was an easy piece of ass. It wasn't like in New York; there weren't too many girls to choose from. That's why I kept her around. You know how it is in our business; people hook up all the time. You do it, too. Don't try to deny it. Does everyone you sleep with mean something to you?"

I hated the lie. Aria meant more to me than anything else in the world. So much, in fact, that I was prepared to kill Marisol in cold blood and rot in jail for the rest of my life to assure her safety. I hoped that if she heard my words that she would see them for the lie that they were. I prayed that she could feel the love that I couldn't speak of without risking her existence. If anyone died today, it wouldn't be Aria. Marisol shrugged as she acknowledged the truth of my statement. Miffed, she crossed her arms over her chest and behaved like a scorned lover waiting for an apology.

"I didn't mean to hurt you and she means nothing to me. If we walk out of here now, this is only assault. I'll get my brother involved and you'll get a slap on the wrist. But if this goes further, you'll go to jail. Then we will never be together. Do you really want that, Marisol? Over someone who has such little significance to us both?"

She mulled over my words. I could tell by her expression that she was torn. She questioned my sincerity. I took another step forward, my hands in front of me, inviting an embrace. If I could just get her to take a few more steps toward me, I could be Aria's savior and Marisol's executioner.

"She killed Lacey."

The words were garbled and labored, but Aria's voice broke the spell I was trying to cast. Marisol turned, rushing toward her. "You bitch!" She had become a raging bull, holding the knife in front of her as she charged toward Aria's battered body. Red filled my vision and everything else lost focus, while rage seeped from my feet and erupted inside of me. I lunged for Marisol, trying to interrupt the blade's route to Aria's jugular, but she slipped through my fingers. I watched in horror as the blade sailed with her hand on a current of malice.

A warning exploded from my lungs. "Aria!"

Aria heeded the warning. As weak as she was, all she could do was turn her head. The blade went into her shoulder and the collision sent her tumbling down the stairs helplessly strapped to the chair.

"Jesus Christ!" The prayer escaped my lips as centripetal force took hold of Aria's body. As I ran toward the stairs, Marisol stood watching. Pleasure filled her face as Aria's body struck the wooden surface of the steps. With each impact, another part of her body was injured. I rushed toward her, pushing Marisol out of the way in my haste to get to Aria. My feet didn't carry me fast enough to intercept the rotating motions and I watched in horror as her body collided with the landing. Her final position left her body at an awkward angle. I couldn't tell if she was breathing.

"What the fuck did you do?"

It was my question, but not my voice. Someone else was here.

Chapter 57

DECLAN

The tone of Paige's voice, which was usually smooth and pleasant, shrilled as she took in the horrific scene. I removed my jacket, rolling it into a ball and lifting Aria's head. She groaned as I moved her. My heart leaped at the sound because I knew she was alive. I stole glances upstairs, volleying my vision between what was going on there and giving my attention to Aria. I couldn't risk Marisol flying down the steps to attack us both. Although my view of the scene was hindered, I saw Paige charge at Marisol. She shouldered her like a linebacker, causing Marisol to lose balance and fall out of sight. I turned my ear toward the upper room, but concentrated my sights on Aria. "Hold on, baby. I've got to get you out of these ropes." She whimpered as I struggled with the knots. Her fingertips fell upon the back of my hand as I untangled the rope. They were freezing cold. After I freed her hand, I took it into mine and rubbed to regain the circulation. She pressed her fingers into my palm.

"I…"

It was too much effort. I wanted Aria to preserve her strength. "I know, baby. Don't talk." Meanwhile, bumps and bangs from above told me that Paige was still fighting Marisol. As I moved my hands to free Aria's ankle, I listened to the raised voices.

"You think your little beach bitch can take what's mine? You should pick your friends more carefully!" Marisol screamed. A slight whistle filled the air, followed by a crash. Pieces of pottery trickled down the top steps. A lamp or a vase became the victim to Marisol's anger.

"You're crazy! I've called the police. They're on their way." Paige's voice was much more composed than when she came into the house. "You're not going to get away with this. They'll lock you up and throw away the key!"

More noises from above led me to believe that Marisol wasn't giving up. I had heard somewhere that people in a fit of rage are unbelievably strong. If that was true, it would explain why Marisol hadn't tired after all the hours spent torturing Aria. A piece of furniture scraped the ceiling above me and a sound escaped one of the women. It sounded like rushing air expelled after a punch in the gut.

"This isn't over!

Vocal strain distorted the statement, so I couldn't tell whether Paige or Marisol said it. I loosened the last binding from across Aria's chest and pressed my lips to her ear. "If you can, put your arms around my neck so I can lift you." She obeyed the whispered request. I slipped one arm beneath her back and the other under her knees. I knew better than to move her, but her breathing was hindered by her awkward position. All I wanted to do was to lift her onto my lap and wait for help to arrive. I eased into a sitting position with my legs stretched out in front of me. Cradling Aria to my chest, I laid her head on my shoulder. Her face was swollen, battered, and quickly bruising. Angry red was giving way to a dark purplish blue. Her lips were split in several places, the blood beginning to clot as she rested. I reached up to stroke her cheek and she flinched. I removed it immediately, running my hand lightly over her leg and arm. Two fingers hung limp, a clear indication that they were broken. As I looked down at her feet, I saw the icy blue color beginning to pink, alerting me that her circulation was returning. She moaned, tearing my heart into pieces. "Shhh. I've got you."

She had just begun to settle when a scream echoed through the nearly empty house. A huge crash followed and I heard the unmistakable sound of glass hitting the patio on the other side of the door. The sound of someone running in the direction of the front door told me that only one person had survived the scuffle. The question was who?

Chapter

58

*M*archelle flew from the house the instant that Marisol and the other woman began to fight. Even though she was comforted by the knowledge that someone had come to aid the woman that Marisol had held captive, panic took over. Flashbacks of her father's torture made her run away. She had removed Marisol's car keys from her purse and snuck out the side entrance of the house. No one noticed her and no one ran after her when she started the engine and quietly inched down the driveway. Once she reached the main road, she floored the accelerator.

Images of beaten men, women, and children taunted her. All of the abuse had been by order of her father. As she looked at her hand on the steering wheel, she remembered the vacant eyes of her father when he had put her hand on the hot stove. Marisol had been her champion that day so long ago, but now their father's black blood had contaminated her. The woman in the chair had been brave. She had taken her injuries and issued no sound. But even stone crumbles to dust when enough pressure is applied and the sound of her sister's victim echoed in her ears. She had to get away. The guilt of leaving Marisol's last victim as she lay dying had eaten away at her soul. With each day, fragments of acceptance had fallen away and now her conscience convinced her to go to the people Marisol had told her to avoid. The police. Marisol had constantly warned her that the authorities would throw her in a cell, rape her, and send her back to Colombia. Marchelle put her hand on the gun in the console. Although Marisol had told her otherwise, Marchelle knew that the weapon was loaded. It was her job to keep the car clean and she knew that Marisol always traveled with a loaded gun, but she didn't know why. She would hide it. She would find someone who spoke Spanish and she would take that person with her to the police to speak for her and rescue the people at the house before Marisol killed them. And if the police tried to rape her as Marisol had said, she would use the gun and take her own life. It was a sin to commit murder; especially to kill yourself, but at least she wouldn't be alone. She would follow Marisol into hell.

Carter disconnected the call. The police and an ambulance were on their way to the house where his brother had gone, but Declan feared that Marisol had escaped. As he stopped at a red light, he collected his scattered thoughts. Declan had repeated Aria's comment to him. Marisol killed Lacey. She had admitted it to Aria. Once Aria healed from her injuries, she would testify against Marisol. A flush of vindication warmed him. As he relished the moment, his attention was diverted by a car flying through the intersection. He blinked in disbelief. The driver was Marisol. The light changed and he followed her. Because of the traffic, she had slowed to the speed limit. He was two cars behind. He turned his cell over and punched 9-1-1.

"Ocean City nine one one."

"This is Carter Sinclair. A person of interest in an attempted murder is traveling on Baltimore Avenue in a white Mercedes, license plate Charlie Bravo Charlie five two eight."

"Where are you, sir?"

"Look. I'm a former Maryland State Trooper on Coastal Highway near the Route 90 Bridge following the suspect. Send back-up now."

Carter hit the *end call* button. Seconds later, the phone rang. "This is Sinclair."

"Carter? Where are you? Where's Declan?" Blake's questions were fired with a clipped tone.

"Declan is with Aria. He said that Marisol admitted she killed Lacey. Aria's in bad shape. She's been stabbed. They're stabilizing her for transport to the hospital."

"Jesus!"

"I'm hanging up, Blake. I don't want to lose Marisol."

"Marisol? I can't imagine what's going through your head, man; but don't do anything stupid. Wait for the police."

"Fuck you, Blake. I am the police."

Carter disconnected the call determined to keep Marisol in his sights. His mood darkened as he kept his eyes on the woman who murdered his wife. No fucking way was he letting her out of his sight. He marked the time and checked the gas gauge without losing sight of her. In his rearview, he saw two cop cars join him on the road. The vehicle in front of him had turned off, so now three law enforcement officials were behind her. One of the officers *whooped* his siren. It was enough to spook her. She sped up. The two police cars took chase and he joined them. Sirens blared and lights flashed while cars pulled off to the side of the road. They raced up the street, crossing over the drawbridge on Assawoman Bay and down Route 50. As she turned toward Assateague Island, her car lurched. It bounced wildly as she tried to straighten the tires and avoid a spin out, then the car bucked over a ditch on the side of the road. Careening through a vacant lot, the white Mercedes resembled a tossed marshmallow. It made loud banging noises as it crashed up and down on the broken concrete and gravel. The axle busted before it came to a stop.

Carter flung the car door open and ran across the lot, deciding against pulling out his gun, lest the other two officers might think he was involved in the crime. They ran toward her also, but Carter reached her first. The airbag had deployed. The woman's face was a portrait in blood. She clutched her chest. He almost didn't notice the gun in her hand. "Put it down, Marisol."

She either didn't hear him or wasn't paying attention. She lifted the gun. He leaned in to reach for it, but she began crying. *"Yo lo siento! Yo lo siento!"* Blood mixed with tears and she turned her face toward him.

He'd seen enough criminals to know that most wore unapologetic expressions, but what he saw in her eyes was sorrow. *What the fuck?*

Brilliant light met a blast as a bullet zinged through the window, the discharge close enough to make his ears ring. Carter hit the ground as he heard one of the officers cry out. Gravel stuck to his cheek as he turned to see blood spurting from the wounded man's shoulder. The other officer pulled out his gun and fired into the car. As Marisol's body fell lifeless, a horn blared into the night.

Chapter 59

DECLAN

As if seated on springs of worry, Aria's mother and I popped out of our seats when the surgeon approached. His expression was as stiff as the white starched jacket he wore, but as the distance between us closed, a smile appeared. My heart and stomach performed a circus act.

"She's in recovery and doing fine."

In unison, Jeannie Cole and I exhaled. I extended my hand to the doctor, my first movement since Aria had disappeared through the operating room doors. As I shook it, I gave him a congratulatory slap on the shoulder.

"Thank you so much." Dabbing at tears, Jeannie expressed the same sentiment and gave him a gentle hug. He waved his hand toward the sitting area in invitation.

"Please."

My world had narrowed, nearly ceasing to exist, when I had released Aria's hand to let the medical professionals do their work. Even though the doctor's initial comment had made me hopeful, his changed expression played with the edges of my peace.

"What is it? What's wrong?" Jeannie's voice held a slight tremble.

"There are some things that you should know," he warned. "The facial lacerations were not deep; just a few stitches were needed. As you guessed, there were a few broken bones: three fingers and her right ankle. Her jaw was dislocated and the cheekbone is badly bruised. However, the puncture wound on her lower abdomen is the worst of the injuries. The knife didn't have a smooth blade. That would have been an easier repair. The jagged cut split as it entered and exited her body. It tore through the lower part of her uterus."

"Oh my God." Jeannie gripped my hand and held tight.

The doctor placed his hand over ours. "We repaired the damage. Her position when she was wounded is what kept her from bleeding out. One of the nurses told me that she was tied to a chair. Is that correct?"

I responded by nodding.

"That's what saved her. Her bent position staunched the blood flow. We did the best repair we could; she has more stitches inside of her body than on the outside. She may be able to carry a child, but she should recover as long as possible. Any pregnancy will be considered high risk, if she's able to become pregnant at all."

I turned to Jeannie. "It doesn't matter. There are other ways to have a child."

The doctor nodded, seemingly satisfied with my answer. "You have the right attitude, Mr. Sinclair, but it's important that she feels the same. Recovery is just as much mental as physical. She'll need a lot of support as she heals."

"I was so afraid when Declan told me that she fell down the stairs," Jeannie interjected. "My mind formed all kinds of scenarios. Her back? Her neck? And her legs? All are okay?"

"Again, the fact that she was bound to that chair helped. Her body has more bruises than not and any movement is going to cause her pain. I've order medication to help with that, but given the circumstances, I'd say she's a lucky girl."

"She's a fighter," I said, looking over at her mother. The comment encouraged her.

Jeannie shrugged matter-of-factly. "That's just Aria. She doesn't know how to give up." The hidden meaning in her comment didn't escape me. I nodded and then turned back to the doctor. "When can we see her?"

"She's still heavily sedated. She did come to for a moment and asked about her friend."

"Yes. Paige." I felt a pang of remorse. I was so concentrated on Aria's critical state that I hadn't asked about her. "She was in the ambulance behind us."

"I'll find her treating physician and get some information for you."

Jeannie interjected. "Yes, please do! She's Aria's best friend and she's like a daughter to me. Her family lives out of town."

"I do know that she's conscious. She said it wasn't necessary to contact anyone. She'll be staying overnight for observation, that much I do know, but I'll send her doctor out to talk to you." He stood and I followed. "I'll tell the nurse to come and take you to the PACU."

As the doctor departed, Carter approached. "Any news?"

"She's going to be okay. We're waiting to see her now. What about on your end? Did you find Marisol?"

Carter looked exhausted. "Yeah. It wasn't good. She had a gun and an officer was hurt. Not fatally, but she's dead." His voice was gravel and grit and the dirt underneath, void of emotion.

My eyes widened. "Holy shit."

Carter shrugged. "It wasn't the end I wanted, but she said something to me before she lifted the gun. I asked someone at the station what it meant and they told me that she said '*I'm so sorry*'. I'm still trying to wrap my head around that. If Marisol was the cold-hearted bitch we all thought she was, why would she say she was sorry?"

"I don't know. Because she was a psycho?" I had no explanation, but Carter's expression still held questions.

"It wasn't just what she said, but how she acted. I saw it in her eyes. She honestly looked like she meant what she said."

I shook my head. "I don't know and I don't care. Marisol can rot in hell for what she did to Aria, and to Lacey."

"I guess." He shrugged again, his head tilting slightly. "Now I'll never get the answers I wanted about Lacey and why she left her on the road."

I placed a consoling hand on his arm. "Maybe it's better you didn't. You might not have liked them."

Chapter 60

DECLAN

A nurse from PACU recovery came out to tell Jeannie and me that we would be able to see Aria in about half an hour. When I asked about Paige, she relayed the room number, so we took the opportunity for a quick visit. I owed her a debt of gratitude that I could never repay. If not for her, Marisol's attention wouldn't have been diverted. As I walked into the room, I was surprised to see Blake sitting at Paige's bedside. I walked past him. Scanning over her, I likened her appearance to that of one of my mother's unfinished cross-stitch projects. Sutures randomly dotted her face and arms. A wrap covered her head. I leaned over the bed. "Hello, lovely lady. Will it hurt if I give you a kiss?"

She smiled in response. "I think you should have someone check your vision, but I'll take a kiss. It isn't every day that I get that kind of offer from the world's most handsome man. I think I might have to milk the attention for a while."

I chuckled. "I don't think you hit your head as hard as they said you did. You're strategizing," I teased.

"Hey, if it worked for you, just think about the possibilities. There are tons of cute doctors walking around."

She batted her eyelashes and Blake clutched his chest. "You're killing me."

"Who are you again?" She answered Blake as her eyes sparkled, a playful smile on her lips. "I'm so sorry. I've hit my head. I can't remember."

I looked between the two of them. "There's nothing wrong with you, Paige. I think you know exactly what you're doing."

Paige's expression grew serious. "How's Aria?"

"The doctor says that she's going to be fine."

Relief unraveled the concern from her expression. "Good." She looked up at me. "I snapped when I went inside of the house. I knew Marisol was jealous of Aria, but…" She didn't complete the thought. "Where is Marisol now?"

"Dead."

Paige's eyes widened as shock changed her expression. "Dead? Oh my God." Her words left her nearly breathless and she brought her hand up to her chest.

I took her other hand and hardened my expression. "You don't need to worry about Marisol. All you have to do is concentrate on getting well. Aria's going to need you." As I looked back, I noticed Blake's expression. His lips had tightened into a thin line, his posture stiff. Except for the frenzy of the media circus that he would have to ringmaster, I couldn't imagine why her death would affect him. He appeared to be angry.

"How?"

"Shot. Apparently she pulled a gun on one of the officers." My comment seemed to stiffen Blake even more. He steeled himself so rigidly that I thought he would snap. I tucked the observation into the back of my mind. I had much more important things to think about. Marisol was no longer my problem.

Chapter

61

D amn him!

Marisol's chest rose and fell with outraged breaths while her pulse rushed her blood through her ears. Acrimony bubbled from a cauldron-sized core filled with hate. Her anger hadn't abated since she had run from the house. Aria would have been dead if he hadn't shown up. And then that other bitch, Aria's friend, one could only hope that they were making her funeral arrangements. Marisol contemplated her next move.

Once she had thrown Paige to the side, the pandemonium that occurred as the woman flew through the glass had given Marisol an opportunity to escape. She had slipped out of the front of the house, rather than through the back. Blood and bodies were scattered there. It would have been a shame to step through a puddle of blood while wearing such beautiful shoes. Declan's car had been open with the keys inside. She doubted he would even miss it. As she had driven away from the house, she saw ambulances rushing toward it. She stayed with traffic, not bringing attention to herself in any way. She had hoped that all they would find were dead women and a grief-stricken man, but there was no way of knowing. She had turned on the radio in the car, but it was too soon for the media to play a report.

The question gnawed at her thoughts. She had to know if she had managed to snuff out the life of her nemesis. After driving around for several hours with no news, the suspense was killing her. She would have sent Marchelle to snoop around, but she couldn't find her. Her sniveling twin was probably hiding in some corner.

"Goddammit!" Marisol said the word aloud as she slammed her hands on the steering wheel. She whipped the car around in the middle of the highway. Horns honked and blared as she wove in and out of traffic. There was only one way to find out. She pointed the car in the direction of the hospital.

Chapter 62

Declan

"Hi, beautiful."

Aria gave me a weak and sleepy smile. As she inched her lips apart to speak, pain infiltrated her face. Her eyes slammed shut in protest as her bottom lip quivered.

"Shhh. Rest. I'm here. So is your mom." Her features relaxed. Seconds later, her breathing evened out, as evidenced by the peaceful rise and fall of her chest. I turned to Jeannie. "I'm taking her home with me." Her drawn brows furrowed her forehead, her tight lips an unspoken protest. "Don't fight me on this, Jeannie. I'll get round-the-clock nurses and whatever else she needs. I'll even get someone to oversee her business until she's fully recovered, but I've made up my mind."

"What if that isn't what she wants?

"Then I'll have to convince her. I'll have to tell her every day that I'm in love with her and I'm not letting her get away from me again." The declaration—the admission of truth—softened her expression and brought a smile to her lips. "I can't live without her."

"She's very headstrong. You might have a fight on your hands."

"Then so be it. I know Aria loves me. I knew it in Hawaii. I was a fool not to fix things while we were there. I won't remake the same mistake." I turned to Aria. Like a bruised and battered Sleeping Beauty, she quietly rested. The effects of exhaustion, anesthesia, and medication intertwined and forced her body into a deep slumber. I couldn't stop staring at her. She was everything in a woman that I could hope for, but never knew I could have. Beautiful and brave made her a deadly combination for my lovesick heart. Aria was the air I breathed, the life that rushed through my veins. If I had a weakness, she was it.

Jeannie Cole was a petite woman, but when it came to protecting Aria, she was an Amazon. She wasn't a pushover. If she had any doubts regarding my sincerity, she didn't voice them. "I'll come over every day," she declared.

I chuckled as I smiled, grateful for her acceptance. "I wouldn't dare try to keep you away."

***

We had sat watching Aria for more than an hour. She drifted in and out of sleep, opening her eyes for only a few seconds and then going back into a deep slumber. I suggested to Jeannie that she go home to get some rest. Once Aria was fully awake, I was confident that she would want to see her mother. Then I could go home, shower, and bring some of her personal things to make her more comfortable. I gingerly removed Aria's hand from mine and placed it on the bed beside her hip. As I stood, I rolled my neck muscles to loosen them and then took a long stretch.

Jeannie hooked her purse over her arm. She came around to the other side of the hospital bed and pressed her lips into Aria's hair. "Love you, sweet girl. I'll be back in the morning." Her whispered affection blanketed my heart with tenderness. She looked up at me.

"C'mon," I tipped my head toward the door. "I'll walk you to the elevator." As we left the room, I pulled the door slightly closed. We took a few steps and Jeannie slipped her hand through my arm. Fatigue was fast setting in and we strolled at a languid pace. "Thanks for being so good to me," I said as I looked straight ahead.

Jeannie kept her eyes in front of her as well. "Treat her right and protect her. She does love you. I'm certain of that."

We reached the elevators and I pushed the button. I turned to Jeannie as I prepared to empty my heart with a confession. The near loss of Aria had structured my priorities. As long as I had her, everything else in my life would fall into its proper place. "I've loved your daughter from the moment I saw her and the more I got to know her, the deeper I fell. I promise, Jeannie, I'll never hurt her again and I'll spend the rest of my life making her happy."

Chapter 63

DECLAN

I made my way back to Aria's room with a blanket tucked under my arm. Upon requesting it, one of the nurses had given me a fresh one from the warming unit. I walked quickly so that the heat wouldn't escape. I pushed on the door and crept in. A flock of nurses had been in and out of Aria's room taking her vital signs and another was with her now. I leaned against the wall and closed my eyes. Exhaustion was quickly corrupting any efforts I made to remain awake until I was able to talk to Aria and tell her of my plans. With my eyes closed, my thoughts began to drift. I could picture us both on the porch, perhaps enjoying one of Aria's favorite things. Coffee. I could nearly smell the mix of the rich aroma with the fragrance of salt air, but as I inhaled the scents from my imaginary scene something was wrong. Instead of the blended scents I expected, the image was contaminated by another fragrance. Something familiar. Something rare. Something expensive.

Something noxious.

My eyes flew wide open. Thoughts fired in rapid succession with observational bullets. The nurse's back was to me. Her hair was tied loosely. Her scrubs were fresh and crisp. The top was something whimsical, the pants an ordinary blue. As my gaze fell lower, something conspicuous struck me. Stilettos. My body reacted. As I sprang into action, I noticed Aria's foot shaking violently. She was giving me a warning the only way she could.

"Get away from her!" I pounced just quick enough to grip her shoulders and throw her to the floor. "Marisol!"

The shock momentarily rendered me incapable of movement as her beady black eyes bore a hole through me. Marisol took advantage of the delay in my reaction and with cat-like reflexes jumped up and dashed toward the other side of Aria's bed. She kept her eyes on me, an evil grin lassoing her lips, as she reached for the IV pole and yanked the tubes from Aria's arm. Alarms beeped and buzzed, piercing the quiet of the nurse's station. I nearly intercepted her, catching her sleeve. She flew in roundhouse motion, punching me in the face. The intentional collision of bone to bone threw me off balance. Using both hands and all of her might, she pushed me from behind. "Go to the bitch, you stupid fuck." Marisol screamed the words and pushed again. "GO!"

The order caused a detonation inside of my head. White light shattered into silver sparkles. I was no longer in the hospital, but on Coastal Highway. Aria wasn't lying in a hospital bed; she was across the street. Her foot had stepped into the road. It wasn't shaking to signal danger. I had called to her, but someone was behind me. I recognized the perfume. It was the same scent that had invaded my nostrils only moments ago. It was the last speck of recall I had before I heard Marisol's voice. When she angrily spat the word out at the top of her lungs. The same word she had used before she pushed me into the highway. The word *GO*.

Marisol had caused the accident. The realization that she was the one responsible for my injuries made me roar with a fury born in hell. My lungs burned as the ungodly sound of my anguished cry escaped. I was a wounded animal, lost in a memory of twisted metal and burning rubber. Pandemonium broke out as nurses, doctors, and other medical professionals ran into the room. All I could feel was the replay of pain, the impact that broke my body and my heart and sent my life repelling down into a gorge of self-destruction. Rage roared through every cell in my being as my mind screamed an instant replay to my limbs. I could feel myself falling, helpless to my affliction and powerless to protect Aria. It was too much. My mind couldn't cope. The flashback was too powerful. I was about to give in to the enveloping darkness as my mind tried to protect itself from shattering into insanity, when I felt iron bands strap around me in a vise-like grip and I heard my brother's strong voice.

"I've got you."

Chapter 64

Marisol ran down one flight of stairs. Most people would have found it impossible to stay calm under such circumstances, but she had plenty of experience dodging paparazzi. The frenzied crowd on the floor above made her confident that no one would notice her absence. Their concentration was on repairing the damage she had done. The hospital would want to avoid liability issues, focusing their efforts on covering their legal asses, not chasing down someone in medical garb. Her plan was to find another disguise and simply waltz out of the hospital doors when the shift changed. She wasn't trapped, merely delayed; once she had removed herself from the facility, she had friends who could get her out of the country. All of her efforts today had produced a disappointing end. Perhaps it was time for a vacation. She drifted in and out of patient rooms, blending in by doing menial tasks such as refilling water glasses. On two occasions, the room had been empty, which had provided the opportunity for her to attempt to contact her sister. Marchelle wasn't answering the phone. Surely someone was watching Declan's car by now, although she had driven onto the hospital grounds without notice. She needed Marchelle to meet her and drive her away from all of the excitement. Marisol ducked into a closet that looked rarely visited and fitted herself into the space between two shelving units. It was as dark as night and had a stale smell, but it served her purpose.

She closed her eyes, picturing the beautiful beaches of Cartagena and Capurgana, thinking this little beach in Maryland paled in comparison to their beauty. Soon she would be in Colombia. She could regroup, make a plan, and form an alibi, perhaps using Marchelle as a scapegoat. She smiled as the image formed of her sister serving in her stead for whatever sentence was required. Marisol used the flashlight on her phone to note the time. More than two hours had passed. She heard no alarm codes over the intercom calling security or rush of bodies careening through hospital floors. The shift was about to change and there would be an abundance of people coming and going. Still no answer from Marchelle. She would have to do this on her own. Marisol backed out of the door, taking a pack of brown paper towels and a container of sanitizer. The key to being inconspicuous was dependent on the ability to blend in. It would be difficult, as she always stood out in a crowd, but it wasn't impossible. Rounded shoulders, chest caved in, and bent knees—the posture of the peons—would render her successful in her quest. The elevator door closed. Marisol pressed herself into the corner, chin to her chest, hair tucked inside of the stolen lab coat. It was long and came below her knees, but it provided a more believable appearance given that her pants and shoes were more career-wear than uniform. The door gave an exhale as the seal released and she pushed out with the herd of people. All were rabid to get through the doors and breathe fresh air and Marisol shared their desire. The sun was shining, inviting her escape. Only a few more steps to the exit. Her hand reached out for the not-fully-closed door as people exited in quick succession. She sucked in a breath, exhausted from the day's events, when a hand roughly clamped down on her shoulder. A twirling motion like a spinning top forced her to look into the hardened expression of Carter Sinclair. His jaw was firm and rigid as he crossed muscular arms across a proud chest. Then two sets of hands gripped her, one from each side, as they captured the top of her arms. She tipped her chin up in an unspoken challenge as Carter's gaze morphed into a dark, threatening glare. With his legs spread apart and feet anchored to the ground, he gave the impression that he would end her life right there if he could.

"Marisol Franzi, you are under arrest for the attempted murder of Aria Cole." His voice was composed of lightning and thunder. "Anything you say can and will be used against you in a court of law. You have the right to an attorney. If you cannot afford an attorney, one will be appointed for you. Do you understand these rights as I have read them to you?"

Her upper lip curled, revealing a snarl. "No. I won't stand for this." She gave a look to each of the officers holding her and attempted to pull her arms from their grasp. Instead, they pulled her hands behind her and thrust each through a loop. It tightened as they pulled, more plastic than metal, and she unsuccessfully jerked them in an attempt to be free. She shot Carter a deathly glare. "You won't get away with this. I want an attorney!"

Carter moved forward, closing the distance, his chest nearly touching her nose. He dwarfed her in stature, close to three times her size, and bent at the waist to respond. His breath was hot, like dragon's fire, the tone incinerating her indignance. "That's where you're wrong, Marisol. I can and I will. As you've made perfectly clear to my family and me, you can't always get what you want."

Chapter 65

Declan

Three Months Later

*N*o way in hell would I ever tire of this view.

I watched Aria as she rested peacefully. Her body had undergone so many changes since the first time I saw her. Her leg peeked out from beneath the sheet, the crisp linen lying just across her thigh. The bruises had faded, the cuts now thin lines in various shades of healing. She looked so fragile in the large bed, but there was nothing about her that defined the word. I gave in to the need to touch her, to reassure myself that having her with me wasn't a figment of my imagination. I sat on the side of the bed and skated my thumb across the back of her hand. Today was going to be a big day for her. I could only hope that she would be pleased. Having almost lost her, I now understood a deeper meaning of the word *treasure*. As a child, I'd always acquainted the word with pirates and gold, but I've come to realize that not all thieves wear red bandanas or black hats and not all treasure is measured by metal. The most precious ones of all are weighed in blood and bone. They live and breathe and can be taken away from you in the span of a heartbeat.

"You're deep in thought." Aria's sleepy voice flitted through my introspection. I raised my hand to her face and she turned her cheek into my palm. She embraced my touch, her eyelashes fluttering against my fingers, as she closed her eyes and smiled.

"I have a surprise for you." Her eyes opened and I sank into the blue depths. The trust in them swelled my heart. "I've invited everyone over later today." Excitement made the blue a little brighter as silver flecks danced in their hues.

"I was beginning to think I was your prisoner. You have been stingy with socializing."

"Only so that you could heal. I didn't want you to overdo it." She scanned my expression and gently nodded. I had sequestered her for only useful purposes, one of which was so that she would be strong enough to endure what I had planned.

"It will be good to see everyone together. Like old times. You're worse than the hospital, limiting my visitors to only one or two." Her smile was mischievous, coordinating perfectly with the gleam in her eyes. "When?"

"Later. I want you to rest and take your time getting ready. I've even brought your breakfast." I shifted so that she could better see the tray.

"Mmmm. Coffee." I had obeyed the unspoken request and made a cup just the way she liked it. She fluffed the pillows behind her so that she could sit up in the bed and pulled her long dark hair to the side. It tumbled over her shoulder, shoving aside the strap that rested there only moments ago. I approached and she took the cup from me, holding it between both of her hands. As the porcelain kissed her lips, I watched as she enjoyed the simple pleasure of that first sip, that fraction of a moment when she closed her eyes as she ingested the first taste of the day. I was hypnotized by the star-shaped scar that undulated as she swallowed. The mark of a beast. "I'm glad you decided to be sociable again. I was beginning to feel like a bird in a gilded cage."

"I still think you should take it easy." Objection hung heavy in my words. Aria was unaware that I'd been planning this night for a month. Her doctor had assured me that she was healing better than he could have hoped, attributing it to her healthy lifestyle. I was excited for the evening, but disguised my feelings so as not to give any details away.

"I'm ready to get out of this room. The doctor said that I could go up and down steps. Somehow I think you sequestered me up here so that you would have me all to yourself."

"Stop." Although I objected to the implication, her tone was playful. While Aria had been in the hospital, I had enlisted her men to come over to the house and make some changes on the second floor. They were more than happy to comply, making two bedrooms into one while transforming a third into a sitting area. All of the sawing, hammering, and painting had been completed before she was released. She was still very weak when she had left the hospital. Her doctor had said that it would be better if she didn't navigate steps, so I carried her up the stairs. She had been as light as a feather in my arms, or was it the adrenaline rush caused by the happiness of having her with me that had lightened her body weight? Nonetheless, once I had deposited her into the most comfortable chair I could find, I managed to keep her on the upper floor for one week more than recommended.

Aria slipped her legs out from beneath the covers and placed her feet on the floor. Bracing the mattress with both of her hands, she pushed to help herself stand. She winced as a cramp tore at her lower abdomen. I jumped up. "Here. Let me help you." I took her arm as she breathed through the pain.

She exhaled and smiled at me. "Thanks. I'm good."

"Maybe I should cancel tonight."

She met my comment with an icy glare that nearly froze me on the spot. "Don't you dare."

I chuckled at her warning. Aria's vicious expression wasn't something I was used to, but whenever she tried to act all badass on me, it made me laugh. "I'll think about it." She pushed my shoulder and went into the bathroom alone. Since the door was closed, I glanced over at her closet. While she had been sleeping, I'd hidden a dress that had been designed for her. Something special to wear tonight. Something to make her feel like a princess.

My princess.

Chapter 66

Aria

I caressed his cheek as we descended the stairs. The new lines that were etched into his handsome face were there because of unfortunate experiences. They enhanced his attractive features and the meaning behind them, as well as the storms we had weathered, made me love him all the more. Everything was quiet when we reached the bottom stair and he let me go to stand on my own. As I started to walk, he blocked the movement and took both of my hands into his.

"I love you. Do you love me?"

I would have laughed, and even playfully answered, but there was something different in his eyes. More contemplative. More severe. I chose my words to meet his depths. "With all of my heart."

"Then stay with me." He drifted down on one knee, holding my left hand and reaching into his pocket with his right. He pulled out a velvet box; the sight of it made my heart melt into a puddle. As he popped open the lid, he turned it toward me for my inspection. A brilliant diamond was nestled in the center of two platinum waves. "I'm asking you to spend every day with me, Aria. I want every sunrise and sunset. Every storm and calm sea. I know how you love being by the water. If you say yes, I'll be your ocean. Stay by my side. Ride the waves with me."

I looked deep into his eyes. For the past few months, we had spent days and nights revisiting issues and sorting things out. We had chosen to leave heartache and blame in our past and concentrate on our future together. What I saw reflected in his gaze was tomorrow's promise. I saw love.

He squeezed my hand. "Say yes. Marry me."

My throat constricted. His declaration tightened my throat with emotional fingers. A barely spoken breath carried my answer. "Yes."

He stood and removed the ring from the box, slipping it on my finger. The fit was perfect, just like him. Declan kissed me long and deep; the lush feeling I received from the intimate connection suddenly made me wish that he would carry me back up to our room. As he pulled back, a devilish grin tugged at his lips. He took my hand and led me around the corner to the main area of the house. The further our steps, the wider his grin. I couldn't remember ever seeing him look so happy. A breeze brushed my skin. Both sets of French doors were wide open, inviting us to take in the landscape. Blue and beige, both outside and in, made the house and the sea seem as one. Our friends watched as I glanced around the room. Typically they were a lively bunch, but they all wore happy smiles. I gave Declan a puzzled look. He pressed his lips to the back of my hand as I looked at him for an explanation. "I'm not giving you a chance to change your mind."

A million butterflies took flight in my stomach as I turned my head to decipher his meaning. I scanned the room a second time, paying more attention to detail. This evening wasn't about a simple dinner party. An army of white candles lit the night, casting a soft light that made the scene warm and inviting. They stood at attention as they decorated the perimeter of the room, the lines of their formation carrying through to the outside porch and into the sand just past the bottom step and onto the beach. My mother moved out from among our friends and I realized that even more people were outside. The dining room table was covered with blue and beige linen. The centerpiece was a three-tiered cake. Creamy shades of vanilla fondant were decorated with starfish and seashells in graduated sizes with a large spindly starfish standing proudly on top.

A wedding.

I felt weak and overwhelmed. I struggled to hold back tears. Like all little girls, I had dreamed of this day, carefully selecting each detail. I had designed my gown, sampled the cake, and carefully selected the guest list. He would be handsome and I would be beautiful, his Prince Charming to my Cinderella. But Declan had removed all choice and taken matters into his own hands, consulting me not once for approval.

"This is for us, baby," he said, waiting for my reaction.

I gave him a look that defied description. How could he have taken liberties with a dream I had never shared? How could he have gotten it all so...

Perfect.

I gave him a gentle nod and leaned into his arm. I had done nothing, but I felt weak. A look of concern crossed his face. I shook my head so slightly that no one but him noticed. He lifted a finger and caught a tear before it passed my cheek.

"He thought of everything." My mother approached, unshed tears in her eyes. "A minister is waiting on the porch." Removing my hand from Declan's arm, she linked it with hers. He leaned over to kiss my cheek and left us to step outside. I floated in the middle of a dream, weightless and high. My mother gave my hand a reassuring pat to assure me that this was real as we followed behind him.

As I stepped out onto the porch, my emotions were hijacked and strapped into the seat of a roller coaster. They ascended toward the top, the face of each person another click in my mind as Declan took my hand at the tip. The climb was scary, but exhilarating, and a mixture of fear and excitement gave me a rush. All I had to do was hold on for the ride. My body, not used to exerting much physical effort, was weakened further as my emotions drained me. Ever sensitive to my waxing and waning strength, Declan made me retreat until something hit my calves. A curtain of people pulled back to reveal a pile of wood and chipped green paint. My eyes misted over as a precious gift came into view, accentuated by fluffy white pillows. The wood was worn, the paint chipped, and the screws holding it together were a little rusty. The irony struck me that it was a perfect representation of the path that Declan and I had traveled to reach this point in our relationship.

"Daddy's chair."

Declan gently tipped my chin, drawing me into his eyes. My heart inflated with helium as my belly reached to lasso it before it spiraled into outer space. The man who had taught me to experience new universes had become the star in my sky. He guided me toward the seat as two of our guests carried a chair of equal size and stature, placing it next to mine. Although unconventional to be married in a seated position, I had come to expect the unexpected where Declan was concerned. Two worlds had collided the day that we met, one beautiful and one plain, only sharing a love for something enjoyed by so many others—coffee. Our coming together was as unusual as beans and water blending to create something perfect; and as we walked our journey, whether refreshing or bitter, it left us craving more. But it would be silly to base a relationship on a morning brew. It wasn't the coffee or the storm or the negatives we had turned into positives. What brought us together was something much more precious. The one thing that we all possess, but can choose to freely give away. A unique treasure that cannot be borrowed, bought, or bartered.

The heart.

He gave me his, I gave him mine, and in doing so, we had a promise of something wonderful.

Our future.

Marisol Epilogue

Clifton T. Perkins Maximum Security Criminal Hospital,
Jessup, Maryland

Marisol sat unmoving on the center of the cot. She had not yet received a response from those she had reached out to, but she still believed that there was hope. She had a network of people, mostly in the shadows, who would carry the details of her incarceration to someone who had the power to help. She vowed that once she was released, she would never allow this type of situation to reoccur. The unflattering prison clothing itched and scratched her skin and she wanted to burn every thread. Although kept in solitary confinement, she felt eyes boring into her as she showered, a right they had taken, but hadn't been granted. She wanted to rip their eyes from their sockets for the theft of the privilege. She had fired the attorney appointed by the State, instead choosing her own. He was as corrupt as she was, but he knew who to contact to put the plan in motion to secure her freedom. Even though her father was dead, there were those who continued his legacy; those who would walk over dead bodies to set a drug lord princess back on her throne. It would happen, she was sure of it, and

those who disgraced her would face payback a thousand times great-
er. It was only a matter of time.

The End

A Note to You from Me

The past nineteen months have been an emotional journey. A beast rocked our family life, and it stole from me the man who held my heart. Just days before his diagnosis with the most aggressive form of brain cancer I had released the fourth book in this series. The moment that the doctors made a confirming diagnosis, all of my efforts to market my books ceased while his fight for life became the center of my world.

Over the next few months, I found that I could not concentrate on writing. I went with my warrior husband to every treatment and became his primary caregiver. I wasn't allowed in the radiation area, so I diverted my attention with online classes. What I discovered was that I had the ability to better my stories. After much thought, I made a risky move. I took all of my books off of the market.

My peers were divided on their opinion of my decision. Many remain so but ultimately; I wanted to be satisfied with the final product.

I am.

It is my hope that you are as well.

XOXO,
DD

P.S. You mean the world to me! Please go to the next page for a way that we can keep in touch.

Like what you've read?

You are cordially invited to be a part of my close circle of friends. You will be privy to exclusive excerpts, deleted scenes, and did I mention gifts and prizes? Join my mailing list at

www.ddlorenzowrites.com

I want to thank you for purchasing and reading my stories, and I value your opinion. I depend on your review. Without them I have no way of knowing if you would like to meet more of my characters and delve deeper into my world. If you would be so kind, please leave your thoughts with the retailer of your purchase and at

http://bit.ly/GoodreadsDDLorenzo.com

Acknowledgments

Mike ~ thank you for sharing your life, love, and dreams with me. You are my hero, now transformed into my angel. Forever my life is changed because of the love we shared.

My loving family and friends ~ thank you for holding me up. Thank you for holding me together. Your support and encouragement kept—and keep—me going.

My sweet little D's ~ Your smiles and laughter are pure magic. They chase away the darkest clouds. You are my heart. I love you a bushel and a peck and a hug around the neck.

Finally, to the talented industry professionals who have worked with me on this project, thank you. Your gifts make my work shine.

About the Author

D.D. Lorenzo aspires every day to be a better writer than she was the day before. From childhood, she has been more an empath than she cared to be. Sensing the emotional connections between family and friends, she wrote her first story when she was six years old. The gift continued into adulthood and with the encouragement of a few *New York Times* Bestselling Authors, she took a leap of faith and published. In her spare time, she loves sinking her toes in the sand on the eastern shores of Maryland and Delaware. She lived a love story with her late husband, Mike, and now considers him her guardian angel. When she isn't writing she enjoys the company of her eclectic family, friends, and her adventurous King Charles Cavalier puppy, Sawyer. The only things she doesn't like are judgmental people and okra. You can find DD on Facebook, Instagram, Twitter, Pinterest, and Goodreads.

Stay connected with D.D.

If you'd like to be part of her communities, check out

https://www.facebook.com/ddlorenzo.author

or join her private FB group

https://www.facebook.com/groups/DDsDivas

Other Titles by D.D. Lorenzo

Depth of Emotion Series

Positive/Negativity (Book One)

Selective/Memory (Book Two)

Here/Now (Book Three)

Same/Difference (Book Four)

Beauty is a Bitch (Book Five)

Made in the USA
Columbia, SC
04 September 2017